"So you found us another cook?" Cody asked.

His uncle Ted nodded, gnawing at his toothpick. "Working on lunch in the cookhouse as we speak."

Relief surged through him. "That's great. I know the hands have been whining about the food. So who did you find?"

"A surprise," Ted said with a grin Cody didn't trust.

"You know I don't like surprises. Just tell me. Clayton's not that big. Please don't tell me you listened to Jonathan and got Vivienne Clayton to come and cook." The city chef would never last on the ranch.

Ted said nothing. Instead he opened the door of the cook shack with a flourish. Cody stepped inside.

And stared in disbelief as the very person he had warned his uncle against now stood in his kitchen.

* * *

Rocky Mountain Heirs:
When the greatest fortune of all is love.

Books by Carolyne Aarsen

Love Inspired

A Bride at Last
The Cowboy's Bride
†*A Family-Style Christmas*
†*A Mother at Heart*
†*A Family at Last*
A Hero for Kelsey
Twin Blessings
Toward Home
Love Is Patient
A Heart's Refuge
Brought Together by Baby
A Silence in the Heart
Any Man of Mine
Yuletide Homecoming

Finally a Family
A Family for Luke
The Matchmaking Pact
Close to Home
Cattleman's Courtship
Cowboy Daddy
The Baby Promise
*The Rancher's Return
The Cowboy's Lady

†*Stealing Home*
*Home to Hartley Creek

CAROLYNE AARSEN

and her husband, Richard, live on a small ranch in northern Alberta, where they have raised four children and numerous foster children and are still raising cattle. Carolyne crafts her stories in an office with a large west-facing window through which she can watch the changing seasons while struggling to make her words obey.

The Cowboy's Lady

CAROLYNE AARSEN

Love Inspired

Special thanks and acknowledgment
are given to Carolyne Aarsen for her participation
in the Rocky Mountain Heirs miniseries

Recycling programs
for this product may
not exist in your area.

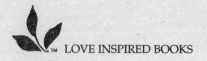

™ LOVE INSPIRED BOOKS

ISBN-13: 978-0-373-81576-0

THE COWBOY'S LADY

Copyright © 2011 by Harlequin Books S.A.

www.LoveInspiredBooks.com

Printed in U.S.A.

Trust in the Lord with all your heart and lean not on your own understanding. In all your ways submit to him and he will make your paths straight.
—*Proverbs* 3:5–6

I'd like to dedicate this book to my amazing fellow authors in this series: Linda Goodnight, Deb Rather a.k.a. Arlene James, Lenora Worth, Roxanne Rustand and Kathryn Springer. It has been a lot of fun working with you all.

Chapter One

She was back where she started.

How many years had she itched to get out of Clayton, Colorado, aka Hicksville? As soon as she graduated from high school, Vivienne Clayton headed for New York to make her name as a gourmet chef.

But here she was. Back in her hometown. And looking for a job at the Cowboy Café.

Oh, the irony!

Vivienne adjusted the black cardigan she put over the white ruffled T-shirt she'd agonized over choosing. She glanced down at the skinny jeans and black flats she'd chosen for her mission. Too dressy? Not dressy enough?

It would be perfect if she were applying for a chef's job at any restaurant in New York.

But for the Cowboy Café?

C'mon, Vivienne, she told herself, finger combing her long hair away from her face. *You're a Cordon Bleu–trained chef. You can rise to any culinary occasion. Rise to this one.*

And before she left the house this morning, her sister Brooke had said she'd be praying for her—for what that was worth. Vivienne wasn't sure God heard prayers anymore.

Back in New York, living in her tiny apartment, she felt like a minuscule mote in the endless humanity filling the city. She doubted God even knew where she was then.

Doubted he even cared that she was back in her hometown now.

Just before she took a step up to the door, a memory intruded. Her as a young girl coming to this selfsame café, hoping to get a job as a waitress, hoping to help out her family after her father passed away.

But that was then. This was now, and now she was taking charge of her life.

Before she could reach for the door, however, it flew open and a teenage girl stormed out, sandy brown hair flowing out behind her, her eyes a smudge of black mascara and green eye shadow, tears coursing down her cheeks.

"I hate the ranch. I hate living there!" she shouted to the tall, broad-shouldered man who came out right behind her, dropping his cowboy hat on his head. "Just because you're my brother doesn't mean you can make me go back."

"Bonnie, now is not the time," the man growled. He slanted an embarrassed glance toward Vivienne.

And to her surprise, Vivienne couldn't look away. Time halted as her heart quickened with an unidentifiable emotion.

He was good-looking—she had to concede that—but something else was happening with her reaction to him. She knew him. Clayton wasn't a large town, and she had grown up here. She held his gaze, searching his hazel eyes, making note of his dark brown hair, glancing over his stubbled cheeks and chin.

"Viv?" he asked, his dark eyebrows shooting together in a frown. "Vivienne Clayton? I heard you were back."

She blinked, trying in vain to pull up something to trigger a memory. But nothing. She lifted her hands as if in surrender. "Sorry, I don't remember who you are."

His eyes grew suddenly hard and he pulled back as if she had slapped him. "And why would you?" he said with a short laugh.

Who was he? And why did she feel they had some history? Some connection? And how come he seemed angry with her?

"So are we going back to your stupid ranch,

Cody?" Bonnie's imperious voice rang out down the street as the man named Cody jerked his gaze away from Vivienne's.

"Just get into the truck," he ordered. "We're leaving right now."

As he walked away, his long legs eating up the distance between him and the young girl, the mention of his name teased recollection out of Vivienne's past. And her face flushed as the memory returned.

It was years ago. When she was still in high school. She had been hanging around after school with her friends, tossing her long blond hair in an effort to gain the attention of the basketball player who had snagged her interest.

Until a tall, lanky senior tapped her lightly on the shoulder, asking if he could talk to her. She turned to him, puzzled as to what he could want.

Working his cowboy hat in his hands as he stood in front of her, Cody Jameson stumbled out a halting request for a date.

Normally, if a senior asked a sophomore to go out, the answer would be an automatic yes. But Vivienne remembered looking at the frayed collar of his shirt and the patch on his faded blue jeans. While the other guys in school all wore loose shirts open over T-shirts, baggy pants and sneakers, Cody still wore narrow blue jeans, shirts with snaps and cowboy boots.

And while Cody wasn't hard on the eyes and seemed like a decent guy, a cowboy from Clayton, Colorado, had never figured in Vivienne's glittering future in the Big Apple.

Hearing her friends giggling at Cody's stumbling invitation didn't help the situation. Though she kind of liked Cody, there was no way she could accept his date in front of them. They'd tease her forever. So she laughed, as well, just to show her friends he didn't matter, and turned him down flat.

After that she saw him from time to time. Once she had hoped to approach him, to apologize, but she never worked up the nerve.

After graduation, he disappeared to his uncle Ted's ranch, where he lived and worked. And when she graduated a few years later, she high-tailed it out of Clayton and never gave him a second thought.

Until now.

Cody Jameson had filled out and grown up, she thought, watching as he pulled his cowboy hat lower on his head before yanking open the truck door for Bonnie, his broad shoulders straining at his shirt.

But he was still a cowboy and she was a city girl, albeit transplanted to Clayton. Just for a while, she reminded herself as she pushed the old memories and history aside. *I just have to stay long enough to fulfill the terms of the will. That's all.*

And for now her biggest concern involved getting a job. Though Brooke liked having her live in the same house and hadn't pushed her older sister to work, Vivienne was too used to pulling her weight. She wanted to be able to pay her share of the bills.

Country music and conversation washed over her as she stepped inside the diner. Kylie Jones, recently engaged to Vivienne's brother Zach, stood by a table of patrons, hands on her hips, her brown ponytail bobbing as she laughed at one of the jokes from the group of old men hunched over the table.

Two stools at the counter were empty, so she walked over to one and sat down.

Then Kylie saw Vivienne and scurried over, grinning. "Welcome back! How was Denver? Busy?"

"Compared to New York, no. But it was fun." She'd gone to Denver to connect with an old friend she'd gone to school with and to give herself some breathing space.

Three months ago her life was on a completely different track. A tiny apartment in New York City. Sous chef in a trendy and up-and-coming restaurant and a boss who was encouraging, fun to work with and very attractive. They had dated a few times. During their last date they had shared hopes and dreams and whispered promises of a future.

When news came of the will and the inheritance, Vivienne wasn't sure she wanted to give up what she had—especially when the money from Grandpa Clayton had so many strings attached. One of which was moving back to Clayton for a year.

Then, shortly after she'd come back from her grandfather's funeral, her boss told her they weren't compatible. Then he quit.

Vivienne's heart was broken. On top of all of this, the new chef was demanding and hypercritical of everything Vivienne did. She began doubting her skills and grew increasingly tentative. Five weeks ago she made a drastic mistake on a menu for a small, exclusive wedding at the restaurant.

And it cost Vivienne her job.

Now she was back in Clayton. No job. No money saved up. No boyfriend.

Back where she started. Looking for work and banking on a maybe.

Kylie grabbed a menu from the old cash register and poked her thumb over her shoulder. "There's an empty space in the back if you prefer to sit there. I have to bus it yet—"

"Sorry, Kylie, I'm not here to eat. I'm, um… well…looking for a job."

A frown wrinkled Kylie's forehead. "A job? But you're getting—"

Vivienne held up a manicured hand, forestalling the next statement. As Zach's fiancée, Kylie would know about the inheritance their grandfather, George Clayton Senior, had given to each of his six grandchildren. Two hundred and fifty thousand dollars was a lot of money no matter where you came from. And the 500 acres of land was a bonus, as well. But all of this would only come to each of them if all six of the cousins showed up by Christmas and then stayed around Clayton for a year.

Trouble was, none of the cousins knew if the sixth, Lucas, would show up in time, if at all. And if she stuck around Clayton for a year, Vivienne still had to find a way to pay off school debt and a credit card she had maxed out while she worked in New York.

"You know I won't get the money unless we all stick around for an entire year," she said with a determined note in her voice. "And until then I still need to eat and pay bills. So I thought I'd see if you had any openings."

Kylie ran a thumbnail along the edge of the menu, biting her lower lip. "We really don't need a waitress," she said slowly.

"I was thinking of the cooking part."

This netted her another frown from Kylie as

she glanced over her shoulder. Vivienne followed her gaze and caught sight of Jerome's lanky frame through the pass-through window as he flipped a burger on the grill, the sizzle of grease and the smell wafting over her at the same time.

Burgers? Really?

Don't be a snob. You need work.

"Um, I'm not sure Gerald or Jerome need any help." Kylie worried at her lower lip, wearing away the pink lipstick she had been wearing. "You'll have to talk to Erin about that."

"Who wants to talk to me?" A woman with red hair and a pencil stuck behind her ear showed up at the cash register beside the seat on which Vivienne had perched. The register chimed as she rang up a total and pulled the bill out of the top.

"I do." Vivienne tossed a glance at an old cowboy limping toward the counter. She had to hurry. Ted Jameson, Cody Jameson's uncle, may walk slow, but she remembered all too well that anything he found out spread through town faster than a wildfire. "I was wondering if you need a cook."

Erin shot her a frown, then grinned as she glanced from Kylie to Vivienne. "This is a joke, right?"

Vivienne squirmed. "No. I'm serious. I need a job."

"But goodness, girl. You're a Cordon Bleu–trained chef. And you're getting your inheritance."

Vivienne resisted the urge to roll her eyes. Who in town *didn't* know about her grandfather's will?

Kylie leaned closer, lowering her voice. "She only gets the money if all the cousins stick around for a year."

Erin nodded, understanding. Then she gave Vivienne an apologetic look. "Sorry, hon. I've got nothing. Jerome and Gerald don't really need any help."

"I can do pies," she offered. "And my mousse cake is so light, it would just float in here."

Erin scratched the side of her head with her index finger. "Arabella does most of my dessert and pastries."

So much for that idea. Vivienne had never thought her own cousin would end up being her competition for work.

"What about working for the resorts over the pass?" Erin suggested, brightening.

"I don't—"

"Her brother Zach would never let her do that," Kylie interjected with a firm shake of her head. "Not after that horrible accident he had to deal with on the road up there. And winter is coming, so the roads would be really bad."

Erin folded the bill she had just printed off.

"Even if she applied and got a job, he'd talk her out of it," Kylie continued, crossing her arms over her chest in a decisive manner, as if she and her fiancée were on the same page.

"So she can't work there," Erin replied.

I'm right here, Vivienne felt like saying as their talk slipped past her.

"Who can't work where?" Ted Jameson had reached the counter at the same time Erin and Kylie had reached their conclusion. His blue eyes looked all the brighter against his tanned skin. A fine network of white lines radiating from his eyes deepened as he frowned down at her. A battered straw cowboy hat sat askew on his head, and the grin he gave her had a few gaps.

"Vivienne—" Erin said.

"—Can't cook at the resorts over the pass," Kylie finished.

"You can't cook?" Ted asked, leaning to one side to pull his wallet out of the back pocket of a pair of blue jeans shiny with grime. Vivienne guessed they hadn't been washed in months.

Mental note. Don't sit in any booth Ted has just sat in.

"I thought you liked to cook," he continued. "Thought you were some fancy chef?"

"That's right," Vivienne said, struggling to

keep the haughty edge out of her voice. "I trained at Le Cordon Bleu in Paris."

Ted eased a few bills out of a wallet thick with cash. "Well, I suppose that means something to somebody."

"It's a very famous cooking school," Kylie explained. "Gourmet cooking, in fact."

"Gourmet, you say?" He snickered as he shoved his wallet in his back pocket. "Hey. That rhymes. I'm a poet."

"And you didn't know it," Kylie finished for him with a happy grin.

"So you really know your way around a kitchen?" Ted asked, snagging a toothpick out of the miniature wooden barrel sitting beside the cash register.

"Yes, I do. I cook very well." This was said with a defensive tone. *Very well* was not a phrase to be used by a graduate of Le Cordon Bleu. Graduates of that famous cooking school were superb. Amazing. Par excellence.

But her confidence had been shaken in the past month. How could things have gone so wrong with the wedding menu? She never had any doubts about her cooking.

Don't go there. That's over. Stick around long enough to get your inheritance. Then you can go back to New York with your head held high and

*your bank account flush. Then you can start your
own restaurant and prove your old boss wrong.*

"And you need a job?"

"Yes. I do."

Ted looked her up and down, as he unwrapped
the toothpick. Vivienne felt like he was assessing
her as he would a prize stud or a bull.

"You look like you have an idea," Kylie
prodded.

A few more people came up behind Ted to pay
their bills. The entry grew crowded.

Ted angled his head to the door as he tucked
the toothpick in his mouth. "Let's chat outside,"
he said to Vivienne.

So she followed Ted across the street to the
park, where he sat down on a picnic bench. Vivienne glanced down at the seat, trying not to make
a face at the bird droppings liberally decorating
the bench. She found a clear spot on the edge and
perched there, hoping she didn't come into contact with any other questionable material.

"So what did you want to talk to me about?"
she asked, crossing her long legs and flipping her
long hair back over her shoulder.

"We'll consider this part of your interview," Ted
said, resting his elbows on the rough wood of the
table.

"Interview?"

"Yep. If it's a cooking job you're looking for, we could sure use you up at the Circle C."

"But that's a ranch," Vivienne said, tucking her hands into the sleeves of her sweater. The sun had drifted behind a cloud and a breeze had picked up, tossing bright yellow leaves around their table, swinging the seats on the swings of the playground beside them. "I'm a gourmet chef."

"Well, yeah. I get that." The toothpick in his mouth migrated from one side to the other.

"I do gourmet cooking for high-end restaurants."

"Sure. Whatever." Ted leaned closer, his gnarled hands folded together, his eyes twinkling at her. "But we need a cook, and from what I hear, you need a cooking job."

Vivienne chewed her lip, her eyes flicking down the street to the grocery store across from the Cowboy Café and the drugstore beside it. She doubted either place was hiring.

The squeaking of the chains from the swings created a melancholy counterpoint to her reality. No job, no skills other than kitchen ones.

She glanced back at Ted, wondering what Cody would think of this setup. "Do you think I would get the job if I applied?"

"Oh, yeah. I'm sure you'd get the job."

"But shouldn't I do a test meal first?"

"If that's what you want." Ted gave her an encouraging grin.

Even as she turned the idea over in her head, Vivienne couldn't stop her mind from moving ahead. Sure, it was cowboys she would be feeding, but surely she didn't have to serve steak and biscuits every day? She could still bring her own brand of cooking to her job. Keep her skills sharp.

"So do I bring my own ingredients? Or is the kitchen fully stocked?" she asked.

"Honey, you bring what you think you'll need and I'll make sure the kitchen is clean and ready for you."

Vivienne couldn't help another look at the grime on the elbows of his shirt, the bits of mud and straw still clinging to his worn cowboy boots.

She made a note to bring her own pail and disinfectant.

"I guess I can show up tomorrow," she said.

"Sounds good." He pressed his hands against the top of the table to get up. "Now I gotta check in on my little girl, Karlee. She works at Hair Today, you know." He pointed a crooked finger at Vivienne's hair. "She could get you set up with a whole new look. She's good."

Vivienne nodded, then held her hand up to stop him. "So just to clarify. I head down Railroad Avenue to get to the Circle C?"

Ted frowned. "You've never been there before?"

She shook her head.

"Really." He rubbed his forefinger alongside his nose in a gesture of puzzlement. "I thought for sure…" He flapped his hand again. "But, yeah, that's right." He pulled a tattered agenda out of his pocket, licked his finger and flicked through the pages. Then he ripped out an empty piece of paper edged with grease. "I'll give you the directions, just in case." He sketched a map with the stub of a pencil.

"And here's where the cookhouse is," Ted said, drawing an arrow, too.

"And how will I know which one is the cookhouse?"

"It's the long, skinny building. The one with the most worn path to it," he said with a chuckle. "Cowboys love their grub."

He gave her the map and she folded it carefully over, trying to avoid the grease stains. "So I'll see you tomorrow," she said.

"You bet." He tipped his hat to her, then eased away from the table. He shook her hand, gave her another gap-toothed grin, then limped across the grass to the other side of the park where Hair Today was located.

Vivienne watched him go, shivering as another breeze created a swirl of orange and yellow leaves around the table. Fall was definitely creeping up, bringing a hint of cold with it. Could she really spend a winter in Clayton stuck out on a ranch in the boonies?

She glanced down at the map in her hand, misgivings eroding her decision.

But what was her alternative? Pound the few streets of town looking for something—anything—to pay her living expenses and her debts? Move back to New York and lose a chance at starting her own restaurant with the money from the inheritance?

But what if Lucas didn't show up in time? Their grandfather's will clearly stipulated that they all had to be around for them all to get their money. Would she be making a wrong career move for nothing?

She shook her head, dislodging her second thoughts. This was an opportunity to keep her cooking skills sharp and make some money.

And for now, she had no other choice.

"So you found us another cook?" Cody hung the halters on the pegs from the tack shed, glancing over his shoulder at Ted. "I'm impressed."

His uncle nodded, gnawing at his toothpick. "Working on lunch in the cookhouse as we speak."

Relief surged through him. "That's great. I know the hands have been whining about the food."

"Delores's grilled cheese sandwiches for lunch and supper only get a man so far," Ted said.

"At least it's food." Cody had been fielding steady complaints about the grub ever since the last cook got fired for just about killing the hands with food poisoning. He'd managed to rope Delores, a hired hand's wife, into cooking. She claimed the only thing she made was reservations. Or grilled cheese sandwiches. So that's what they'd been eating. "So who did you find?"

"A surprise," Ted said with a grin Cody didn't trust.

"You know I don't like surprises. Just tell me. Clayton's not that big." He stopped and put his hand on Ted's shoulder. "Is it Arabella? Did you talk her into coming?" He could hardly believe his luck. Just thinking about Arabella's pies and pastries got his mouth watering.

Ted angled him an "Are you kidding" look as he limped toward the cook shack. "Woman's got triplets and takes care of that Jasmine girl. As if she'd have time to come out and cook for us."

"So who *did* you get? Please don't tell me you listened to Jonathan and got Vivienne Clayton to come and cook."

Ted said nothing. Instead he opened the door of the cook shack with a flourish. Cody stepped inside.

And stared in disbelief as the very person he had warned his uncle against now stood in his kitchen.

Vivienne wore a tall chef's hat and a white smock and apron. She stood at the stove, her back to them, stirring something smelling, for lack of a better word, weird.

What kind of joke was Ted playing? He yanked his hat off and slapped it against his thigh. He didn't have time for this kind of malarkey. Too many things on the go and hired hands who grew more grumbly with each grilled cheese sandwich they had to choke down.

Vivienne wiped her hands on a cloth lying beside the stove and gave Cody a quick smile, a dimple flashing in one cheek. "Thanks for giving me this opportunity," she said, holding out her hand.

Under that goofy looking hat, her hair was pulled back in a shining ponytail, low on her neck. Her cheeks were flushed, her eyes bright and her cheekbones as beautiful as ever.

She looked even more amazing than she had in high school.

He caught himself, frustrated with how easily she brought back feelings he thought he'd dealt with years ago.

You're not some dumb, love-struck senior anymore. You've lost a wife and—

He stopped his thoughts there. He couldn't go to that dark place. Not now. Not ever.

"What is going on here?" he said, giving her

hand a perfunctory shake. He shot an angry glance at Ted, who lifted his shoulders in a vague shrug.

"I'd like to go over the menu with you, to see what you and your uncle think of my choices," Vivienne said, gesturing toward the stove. She pulled off her hat and whipped off the smock to reveal a black dress with no sleeves and some kind of shiny brooch pinned to one shoulder. "I hoped to have everything ready for my presentation, but you came earlier than I had anticipated."

He didn't want to look at her. "Menu?"

"Yes. For my test meal?"

"Test meal?" He felt like slapping himself on the head. He sounded like some robotic moron.

"Pauley Clayton doesn't carry much of what I needed in the grocery store, but the best chefs can and do improvise." She gave a quick laugh, her eyes flicking from him to Ted.

"I thought we could start with a spinach salad with spiced walnuts and pears and a light vinaigrette followed by glazed pears and a filet mignon with red wine tarragon sauce. I'd like to serve the filet with a reduction made from the pears, but only if you agree." Cody felt bombarded by words and terms he knew nothing about.

Which made him feel stupid.

Which, in turn, made him angry, mostly because it was Vivienne Clayton he felt stupid in front of.

"That sounds like something for a restaurant, not cowboys," he said.

Vivienne lifted her shoulder in a vague shrug. "Cowboys can enjoy gourmet cooking, too."

"Gourmet? Not likely."

Ted grabbed him and gave him a half turn. "You'd sooner eat grilled cheese sandwiches for breakfast, lunch and supper?" he asked, turning, as well, so his back was to Vivienne and he was facing Cody.

"I'd sooner eat ordinary food."

Ted yanked on his arm to pull him closer. "We could use some decent food here," he muttered. "I think we should hire her."

Before Cody could reply, Vivienne handed him and Ted each a plate with half a pear sitting on a leaf of lettuce, and the whole business was sprinkled with nuts.

"Why don't you give this a taste and tell me what you think," Vivienne was saying, "and I'll get the steak ready."

Cody looked from the pear all fancied up to Vivienne. Gold hoops hung from her ears, and her eyes had that smudgy look Bonnie was always trying to create with endless pots of makeup and tubes of mascara.

She looked exactly like she did in high school.

Fancy. Unapproachable. The epitome of the same city girl Tabitha, his wife, had been. Someone who couldn't live out here.

His heart hardened at the memory. He wasn't going there again. Girls like Tabitha and Vivienne didn't belong on a ranch. They couldn't handle the isolation and the stress.

"Sorry you wasted your time coming, Miss Clayton," Cody said, clenching the brim of his battered cowboy hat. "But we're not hiring you."

Then he spun around on one booted heel and left.

Chapter Two

Not hiring her?

He hadn't even given her a decent chance.

"Cody. Hold on," Ted called out.

Vivienne pressed her hands together, trying to keep the panic at bay.

Cody stopped and slowly turned around, his mouth pressed into a thin line, his eyes narrowed. Vivienne stifled the tiny frisson of fear at his belligerent look as she took a long breath.

"We need a cook," Ted said.

"I need someone who can do beans, beef and biscuits. Not…*that*." He waved a dismissive hand at the pears that, Vivienne thought, had turned out very well considering the number of ingredients she'd had to improvise on.

She wanted to be upset with Cody's dismissive attitude, but she couldn't.

Because after speaking with Ted, on a whim,

she walked around town talking to the various businesses. No one was hiring. Not the flower shop. Not Hair Today, the only beauty salon in town. Not the post office or any of the schools. She had even, out of desperation, tried the feed supply store, but Gene Jones, the proprietor, wasn't looking for help either.

The town of Clayton had been dying a slow death even when she lived there. Now, even with the reopening of the Lucky Lady Silver Mine, it was worse. This job was her only chance at making some money while she waited for the inheritance.

Which will only come through if Lucas shows up.

She smothered the errant thought. Lucas had been informed of what was at stake. He would show up.

Ted turned to her and set his hands on his hips. "This is real nice, but would you be willing to cook simpler food?"

Vivienne set the pear down, disappointment vying with practicality. "It's not what I was trained to do."

"But you can do that," Ted insisted.

"I'm a professional chef…" As her words faded off, so did her anticipation at the thought of this job. Gourmet cooking was what she loved. What she was best at. "I suppose I could do what was required of me," she continued.

Cody pulled on his chin with one hand as if this answer didn't satisfy him either. "I'm still not sure—"

"She can go over the menus with us and make sure we think it's okay," Ted insisted.

Cody fiddled with his hat, his teeth working at one corner of his mouth. "I don't think she's the right person for the job."

"We got no one else," Ted insisted. "We kind of need her."

That Ted had to argue Cody into hiring her raised Vivienne's ire. Sure she wasn't a beans-and-bacon cook, but she was, as she had pointed out to Ted, a professional cook. And the thought that someone didn't want to hire her made her angry.

And, perversely, made her want the job even more.

"I'd like a chance," she said quietly.

Vivienne watched Cody's face, trying to get a read on where he was going. Then he looked at her, and as their gazes meshed Vivienne caught a glimpse of the young man who had asked her out all those years ago. Then his features tightened and any trace of that Cody Jameson disappeared, replaced by this hard-looking, uncompromising man.

"We need someone who isn't afraid of hard work," he said, his voice gruff as he addressed her. "We need someone who can live out on a ranch for weeks at a time and not think they're in the middle of nowhere."

Which, as far as Vivienne was concerned, was exactly where they were. But she sensed from the intensity in Cody's voice that her comment wouldn't be welcome.

"I need someone who can live out here when storms blow into town and cut us off from civilization for days at a time," Cody continued. "Do you think you could do that?" His voice had taken on a puzzling, belligerent tone, but even as she held his stern gaze she tried not to wince at the thought of being stranded up here.

"I...think I could do it." She lifted her chin and injected a note of steel in her voice. "I know I can."

It was only a year, she reminded herself, even as her knocking heart belied her confident tone. Three hundred and sixty-five days out here was a small price to pay for a quarter of a million dollars. And maybe more, once she sold the land that was part of the inheritance.

After that, New York and her new restaurant.

Keep your eye on the prize, she reminded herself. *This is only a necessary detour.*

Cody's gaze locked with hers, his hazel eyes

probing, as if trying to find a weakness. She held him look for look, but as she did, her heart did a little unexpected flutter at his attention. She swallowed, willing the emotion away.

He's good-looking. It's a normal reaction, she reminded herself, forcing herself to keep holding his gaze.

He's going to be your boss.

"No one else wants to live out here," Ted said. "I think we should hire her."

Vivienne caught the angry look Cody shot his uncle. Obviously, Mr. Jameson wasn't happy with Ted.

"I'm okay with this," Vivienne said, stilling the threatening note of panic. She'd just have to get creative. Maybe take out a loan to pay off her other debts. Sell some stuff. Live cheap.

"Look, Cody, you make the decision. You know where I stand. I'll be out at the horse pen," Ted said. He dropped his hat back on his head and spun on his heel.

After he left, Cody shoved one hand through his thick brown hair and blew out a sigh.

"We're not looking for gourmet cooking or anything even close to that. I'm just looking for—"

"Someone who can do beans and biscuits." Vivienne gave him a quick smile to counteract the faintly bitter note in her voice. "I get that."

She held her head high. She needed this job, but she wasn't begging.

Cody dragged his hand over his chin, still holding her gaze as if testing her.

"It's not just that," he said, his voice grim. "Like I said, it's a hard life out here. And if I think you can't hack it, you're down the road. I'm not risking anyone's well-being again."

She wondered what he meant by "again," but before she could ask, he continued. "You got the job, okay?" he said with a dismissive wave of his hand at the food she had so carefully prepared. "Just don't get carried away with that fancy stuff."

Don't get angry. Just smile and nod. You've got work for now.

"Thank you," she said, unable to keep the prim tone out of her voice. "You won't be sorry."

Cody's glance ticked over her hair, her dress and her high-heeled shoes that she had slipped on before he came. All in an effort to impress a boss who, it seemed, wasn't impressed.

"I'm not so sure about that," he said grimly.

Then the door of the cookhouse burst open and the young girl Vivienne had seen Cody with in town launched herself into the room. Cody's head snapped around and Vivienne saw a look of frustration and…was that fear?…flit across his face.

"Where's my makeup?" she said, pointing an

accusing finger at Cody's chest. "What did you do with it?"

"Why do you think I did anything with it?" Cody asked, dropping his hat back on his head and tugging the brim down.

"I know you hate it when I wear makeup." The girl's voice grew even more shrill, but then her eyes shifted past Cody. She frowned, pointing a crimson-tipped finger at Vivienne, suddenly distracted by her presence. "Isn't that the woman you were talking to at the diner? Why is she here?"

Cody's broad shoulders lifted in a sigh as he clenched his fists. "This is Vivienne Clayton. Vivienne, this is my little sister, Bonnie."

Bonnie's heavily made-up eyes narrowed and Vivienne understood Cody's difficulties with his sister's beauty regimen. The girl could use a lighter hand with the eyeliner and the mascara. And those bloodred lips. Way too harsh for her coloring and age.

"Vivienne Clayton?" Bonnie took a step closer, her frown deepening. "Are you related to all those Claytons who are coming back to town just for the money?"

Vivienne smiled, choosing to ignore her insult. "I'm George Clayton's granddaughter, yes. And George Junior and Marion were my parents."

"Uncle Ted said you were from New York,"

Bonnie added, her dark-ringed eyes holding hers. Then Bonnie looked down at Vivienne's shoes and her eyes grew wide. "The soles of your shoes. They're red. Are they made by—"

"Christian Louboutin? Yes." She held up her foot, angling it so Bonnie could see the signature red leather soles on her black pumps. "I bought them at Saks." They had cost her a ridiculous amount of money, but they were her first purchase with her first paycheck. And a down payment on a promise she'd made to herself to bury her country roots deep in her past. She was now a New Yorker. And the shoes told people she was going somewhere, which was all the way to the top of her profession.

Bonnie's face beamed at the sight. "Seriously?" she breathed. "You've shopped at Saks?"

"Yes. And Bergdorf Goodman." Never bought anything there, but Bonnie didn't need to know that. Now she was obviously impressed and Vivienne felt the little bit of her self-worth, chipped away by Cody's easy dismissal of her work, restored.

"That supposed to mean something?" Cody asked.

Bonnie looked Vivienne over more carefully. "Do you do your own makeup?"

"Of course I do."

"Could you teach me?"

"Miss Clayton is here to work," Cody snapped. "She won't have time to fool around with girlie stuff like makeup."

Bonnie pushed out a heavy sigh, then turned and stomped out of the cookhouse. As she left, Cody turned back to Vivienne. "Just so you know, I'd prefer it if you keep your distance from my sister."

Annoyance vibrated through her. "I realize I'm here to work, but may I ask why?"

Cody adjusted his hat on his head, then he looked down at her, his eyes narrowed again. "My sister is only fourteen, and she is my responsibility while my parents are overseas. I take that responsibility seriously. I don't want her turning out… I don't want her getting all flighty and full of highfalutin ideas."

Vivienne's spine stiffened so quickly that she was surprised she didn't hear a snap. "And you think I'll give her those highfalutin ideas?" The chill in her voice was a mistake, but she resented the implication that she would be a bad influence on his little sister.

Cody gave a pointed glance at the shoes she had recently shown off. "Living out on the ranch here is hard, and it's not for prissy city girls."

And before she could protest that comment,

he strode out of the cookhouse, the echo of his booted feet on the wooden floor underlining his comment.

As the door shut behind him, relief mixed with puzzlement drifted through her.

She got the job. Not the gourmet cooking job she'd hoped to get, but a job nonetheless.

As to living out here with Cody Jameson watching her every move?

It would work, she told herself, smoothing her sweaty palms over her skirt. She would make it work.

Her gaze flicked to the window over the large double sinks. Through the fly-specked glass she saw pastures, then hills, then mountains.

And not a house, or a road or any other sign of civilization. She shivered again, wondering if she had what it took to stay out here.

"I still can't believe my big sister will be living out on a ranch with cows and horses and no department store within a hundred-mile radius." Brooke dropped another empty suitcase on the pink-and-white checked quilt and unzipped it, her long blond hair swinging over her cheeks. She flashed Vivienne a cheeky grin, her dark blue eyes sparkling with humor. "Sure you won't suffer from shopping withdrawal?"

Vivienne glanced around the bedroom of their

family home remembering pillow fights between her, Brooke and Zach. She thought of the time Zach had found a snake and threatened to put it in her bed. She smiled as she rolled up a pair of socks. Since coming home, she'd been assailed by memories, many of them happy. Maybe being back in Clayton wouldn't be so bad. She turned her attention to Brooke and her skepticism. "Give me some credit, sis. I grew up in this town."

"And when you weren't at Hair Today buying yet another bottle of hair product, you were forever grazing through old fashion magazines Mrs. Donalda brought into the library specially for you." Brooke held up a pair of distressed blue jeans. "I can't imagine what Cody would think about these."

"I highly doubt he would even notice. They're just blue jeans."

Brooke found the heavy cardboard price tag still dangling from a leather string attached to the button and whistled. "I've paid this much to put tires on my car."

"They are renowned for their good fit and quality." Vivienne grabbed the offending pants from her sister, curbing a surge of guilt at how much she had paid for them. She bought them on a self-indulgent pity splurge. After a particularly brutal dressing-down from her new boss, which came on the heels of her boyfriend breaking up with her because, in his words, "We are on different levels," whatever that meant. "And I wouldn't have bought them if I knew I'd be out of work a week later."

"Still, I never thought I'd see the day that someone who would pitch a fit if she broke a nail would end up cooking on a ranch in Clayton."

"I'm hoping I'm a little older and wiser now," Vivienne said, closing the suitcase and zipping it shut.

"With a lot more clothes and makeup." Brooke pulled up the handle for the suitcase and grabbed Vivienne's oversize cosmetic bag.

"Speaking of makeup, what's with Cody and his little sister?" Vivienne followed her sister out of the bedroom, bumping the cases down the narrow stairs.

"Okay, that leap in logic makes perfect sense," Brooke joked.

"Work with me, sis. Bonnie asked me to help her with makeup and I thought Cody was going to have a coronary. He told me specifically to stay away from her." Vivienne grunted as she got the last suitcase to the bottom of the stairs. "I get the impression he thinks I'm a bad influence."

Brooke shrugged as she rolled the suitcase through the living room. "From what I hear, Cody is pretty protective of his little sister, though

I'm not sure why he would think you're a bad influence." She shot a mischievous glance over her shoulder. "Unless you've picked up some evil vices in New York or Paris I've never known about."

Vivienne was about to give her sister a snippy retort, but the front door burst open and a little boy came toddling through, his little feet pumping as he headed directly to Brooke. He had a baseball cap on backward and his T-shirt was stained with chocolate, as was his ear-to-ear grin.

"Book. Book," he babbled, reaching up for her.

"A.J., stop running," she heard a deep voice call out from behind him.

Brooke's face softened as she let go of her sister's suitcase and bent over to pick up the son of her now-fiancé.

Gabe Wesson stepped into the house and, without breaking stride, walked straight to Brooke.

Vivienne felt a twinge of envy as she watched this tall, smiling man rest his hand on her sister's shoulder, then bend over and brush a light kiss over her mouth. Though she hadn't been around when Brooke and Gabe started dating, it hadn't been difficult to hear the change in her sister's voice whenever she called. And when she met Gabe and his little boy, A.J., ten days ago when she moved back into the old frame house she and her siblings had grown up in, she understood why.

A.J., now secure in Brooke's arms, batted his father's face with one chubby hand, his grin even wider.

Gabe dragged his attention away from Brooke and A.J. and frowned as he saw the suitcases surrounding the two of them. "So who's moving out?"

"Vivienne got a job on the Circle C. Working as a cook." Brooke shifted A.J. in her arms, giving him a quick hug.

Gabe's one eyebrow lifted in disbelief. "Really?" he drawled, his incredulous tone telegraphing his opinion of that situation.

"What? You think I can't do that?" Vivienne asked, planting a hand on her hip.

Gabe raised his hand. "Sorry. Wasn't implying anything. It's just you lived in New York, and I can't see you cooking on a ranch—"

Brooke placed a fingertip on his lips. "And you should stop now," she said with a wry smile.

"A good chef can adapt the menu to the patrons," Vivienne said, grabbing a suitcase handle in each hand and lifting her chin in defiance.

"Of course you can," Gabe said with a placating tone, reaching for the other suitcases. "And it looks like you're well equipped to head into the fray." He grunted as he dragged the suitcases down the stairs, Brooke and A.J. right behind. Vivienne brought up the rear, then groaned as a deputy sheriff's car pulled up in front of hers. Great. Just what she needed. More comments from yet another family member.

Zach Clayton eased himself out of the car, and when he saw Gabe toting the suitcases, he frowned.

"Who's going on safari?" he said, sauntering toward them.

"If I have to hear one more comment about how many suitcases I've packed or doubts about how I'll survive on that ranch, I'm hitting somebody," Vivienne muttered, her suitcase bumping over the sidewalk to the waiting car.

"No hitting," A.J. cried out, sounding alarmed.

Brooke patted his back soothingly. "Aunty Vivienne was just teasing, honey." She shot her a questioning glance. "Weren't you?"

"Barely."

"So, my little sis is going to be a ranch cook," Zach said as he helped Gabe heave one of her heavier suitcases into the trunk of her car. "Great advertisement for that fancy cooking school you went to."

Vivienne ignored him as she opened the back door of her car and laid her smaller suitcases inside. "I like how everyone is so confident of my abilities and so supportive of my decision to actually make some money while I'm waiting for Grandpa's money to come through," she snapped as she slammed the car door shut. "I'd like to think it shouldn't be hard to feed a bunch of cowboys. I'm not the prima donna everyone seems to think I am."

She spun around and faced a sheepish-looking Zach and equally embarrassed Gabe.

"Sorry, sis," Zach said, with a light shrug. "Just having some fun with you. We know you're an amazing cook, and that's why it seems like a stretch to see you working out there."

Vivienne knew that and she knew she was being touchy. She also knew her lack of confidence was tied up in the reason she was fired from her previous job.

"Well, I could be working at the resorts—"

Zach held up a hand. "Not a chance, girl. That pass over the mountains to get there is too dangerous."

In spite of her pique with her family, Vivienne felt a flush of affection at her brother's protectiveness. She knew it was because he cared, and it had been a while since she'd had that.

"Anyhow, this is what I chose to do," she said, tempering her stern tone with a smile. "And I'm sure I'll be seeing you all again."

Zach pushed his hat back on his head and heaved out a sigh. "That's one of the other reasons I came here. I still haven't heard anything more from that private investigator I hired to find out what's happening with Lucas. He said he would let me know if I should send in help, but nothing. I wish I knew what to do."

"Our mother would say that we should pray," Vivienne said with a melancholy tone, leaning back against the car. She hadn't prayed in years. Not since she left Clayton. As far as she was concerned, God had died when her mother had. She hadn't talked to Him since.

"I have been," Brooke said, cuddling A.J. close as if to protect him from the trouble Lucas was involved in. The information the family had received so far was that their cousin was trying to rescue a child orphaned by a drug gang deep in the Everglades. The bits of information were confusing and frightening and no one knew what they could or should do. Lucas wasn't in direct contact with any of them.

"If I don't hear anything in the next week or so, I'll have to make a decision about getting the police in Florida involved," Zach said, heaving a heavy sigh.

Vivienne wished she knew what to do to help her brother and Lucas. Zach had always been the one to take care of her and Brooke. Their father, distracted by work and the ongoing feud with his uncle Samuel's side of the family, was an absent father. And when he died in a car accident that also killed his brother—their uncle Vern—Zach had taken the role of protector to Vivienne and Brooke. It had made him older than his years, but it had also brought the three very close.

"Should I take this job then?" she asked, suddenly concerned. "Or should I stay around to help find Lucas?"

Zach gave her a tight smile and shook his head. "There's not much any of us can do, sis. So just go and work. We'll keep you informed."

"I can come back whenever you need me," she said. She suspected that Cody Jameson might not mind if she decided to quit. He seemed reluctant enough to hire her.

Zach patted her shoulder. "We'll keep in touch. Cook good at that ranch and make us Claytons proud," he said, giving her a quick, hard hug.

The various paraphernalia of his police belt dug into her waist as she hugged him back, its heft and weight a grim reminder of Zach's ongoing responsibilities as deputy sheriff of the town.

Then he strode back to his car and was gone.

Vivienne watched him go, then turned to her sister and Gabe. "I should leave, as well." She hugged her sister and gave A.J.'s cheek a quick stroke. "Love you, little guy."

"You'll stay in touch?" Brooke asked, shifting A.J. to her other hip like a seasoned mother. She had grown up quickly in the past few months, Vivienne thought. Her *little* sister no longer.

"I'll be back for groceries sometime or other," Vivienne assured her. "I'll contact you then. Find out what's happening with Mei and Lucas."

Brooke gave her another hug, Gabe flashed her a quick smile, and then Vivienne was in her car and pulling away from the curb. In her rear-view mirror, she saw Gabe drop his arm around Brooke's shoulder and pull her close. The domestic scene tugged at her heart, and again Vivienne felt a surge of envy blended with joy for her sister's happiness.

Would she ever find what Brooke and Gabe seemed to have?

Chapter Three

"Where are you going?" Cody called out to his newest hired hand, Bryce, as he walked toward the cookhouse. "Your horse needs to be brushed yet."

The young boy turned and then dropped his gloved hands on his narrow hips, brown hair hanging in his eyes. "I'm beat. I'm hungry and tired from riding all day. My horse is fine."

And with that he spun around, skinny arms pumping as he ran off.

Cody pressed his lips together, sending up a quick prayer for patience, which was immediately followed by guilt. Lately his prayers were the "Help me, help me" kind sent up in a rush between getting the horses ready for the roundup, getting the last batches of hay hauled and trying to keep his sister from driving him crazy. He hadn't had time for proper devotions in weeks. He just prayed God understood.

Cody sighed as he dismounted, his own legs stiff from riding all day. He should insist the boy do things the right way, but he was new and Cody didn't have the energy to follow through.

Not after spending almost twelve hours in the saddle sorting through the first batch of cows and calves and getting them ready to move in a couple of weeks.

"Why's Bryce heading for grub?" Ted grunted as he swung his leg over the saddle. "Didn't see him brush his horse down."

"He says he's tired."

"Aren't we all? And you've been working since five o'clock. Kid needs an attitude adjustment."

"He's willing to live out here for ten days at a time, so I put up with him." Cody led his and Bryce's horse to the tack shed, the slow thud of the horses' hooves telegraphing their own weariness.

"And hang out with spineless Les Clayton and that no-account Billy Dean Harris when he's not working."

Which made Cody think of another Clayton now inhabiting the place. Vivienne had come to the ranch last night, dragging enough suitcases to outfit every woman in town. But he hadn't had time to talk to her. Instead he got Cade, her cousin on the other side of the Clayton family, to help her.

"As long as Bryce is working for me when he's here, I can't tell him who to hang out with," Cody replied.

"Food smells good," Ted exalted as he pulled the halter off his horse. "Wonder what Vivienne whipped up for supper. Bet it's a whole lot better than grilled cheese sandwiches."

"She better not be making some fancy stuff we can't choke down" was all Cody said, jerking on the saddle's cinch. He still felt like he'd been railroaded into hiring Vivienne. And Ted's constant singing of her praises all day didn't help either. It was annoying.

"Didn't see you for breakfast." Uncle Ted let his horse spit out the bit and hung the bridle over his arm. "You weren't hungry?"

"Had things to do."

"Seems to me like you're avoiding our new cook," he said with a knowing grin.

Cody heaved the saddle off the horse and moved to Bryce's. "You know how busy I am."

"You've got to learn to delegate more. Life isn't just work. And now there's a pretty new cook on the ranch." He winked. "And I heard she's single. You might want to make time for her."

Cody didn't bother responding to Uncle Ted's blatant comments. In the distance a coyote sent up a lonely shivering wail into the cool evening air. But he heard no replying howl.

"It's been almost four years since Tabitha," his uncle said, his voice quiet.

Cody clenched the brush, knowing exactly where Ted was heading.

"You've been pushing yourself since then, working every hour of the day, going nonstop." Ted kept his voice low, as if he knew he had to approach this subject with caution. "Tabitha is gone, and you can't change that."

Cody walked over to Bryce's horse and started brushing him but said nothing. He didn't want to talk about his former wife. Though he missed Tabitha, her betrayal had hurt him more than her passing had. They'd been drifting apart for months before she took off from the ranch.

"So now Vivienne Clayton is cooking here," the older rancher continued, "and I think that's a good thing."

Cody snapped his head around, glaring at his uncle. He should have known his partner wasn't trying to be sympathetic and understanding. Should have known that Uncle Ted always, always had a plan.

"I only hired her 'cause I had no choice, thanks to you," Cody said, wanting to stop Ted mid-matchmaking. "As for her cooking here, she's a Clayton, and she's only hanging around long enough to collect the money that old miser George left her. Once that happens, she's back to New York where she belongs, far as I know. I would be surprised if she sticks it out here longer than a week." He stopped, realizing how defensive he sounded.

Ted led his horse to the corral. "Why don't you like her? I heard you two were an item a time back," he called out over the screeching of the opening gate.

That Ted. He just never let up.

"We were never an item." Cody's movements were brisk as he finished brushing off Bryce's horse.

"But I thought—"

"Look, Uncle Ted, you're my partner, not my life coach." As soon as he spoke the words, Cody wished he could take them back. It was thanks to his uncle he even had a stake in the Circle C. Uncle Ted had only one daughter, Karlee, who had no interest in ranching and lived in town. Ted had taken Cody in during the many trips his missionary parents made overseas and instilled in him a love of the land and a love of ranching.

One of Cody's first memories was of Ted helping him onto a horse and leading him around the corral.

His uncle knew more about Cody than even his

parents did. He knew Cody had a "thing" once upon a time for Vivienne Clayton. Ted just didn't know how flatly Vivienne had turned him down. Cody had been too humiliated to give those details out and had let Ted believe something was brewing with him and "that gorgeous Clayton gal," as Ted insisted on calling her.

"I'm sorry," Cody said quietly, staring over the back of the horse at the darkening sky, unable to meet Ted's gaze. "I shouldn't have said that. It's just, well, I've got Bonnie driving me crazy with wanting to move closer to the center of town and we've the gather to take care of and hay to haul..." He let the sentence drift off. Too much to deal with. Too much to think about.

"It's okay." Ted untied Cody's horse and led him to the corral, as well. "I get it."

"I hope you do," Cody said quietly. "Vivienne Clayton is just the cook here. Nothing else."

"Sure. Of course."

"She's a city girl and always will be now." Just like Tabitha was.

"Yup. I hear ya."

Cody shot his uncle a warning glance as he put Bryce's horse away, but Ted was already through the gate, obviously lured on by the mouth-watering smells drifting from the cookhouse. "You coming?" Ted called over his shoulder.

"Yeah. In a bit." Reluctance kept him back, watching the horses rolling in the dirt, grunting with satisfaction as their legs flailed awkwardly in the air.

His stomach rumbled and he knew he couldn't put off going to the cookhouse any longer.

Trouble was, Uncle Ted had hit on a nerve.

Vivienne Clayton looked as beautiful as he remembered, and in spite of what he'd had to deal with, she still held a certain fascination.

You're older, wiser. She was just a high school crush.

He straightened his shoulders, told himself to man up and followed his uncle across the yard.

But before he could get into the cookhouse, the door slammed open and one of his hired hands, Dover, stormed down the stairs, grumbling as he went.

"What's the matter?" Cody asked, catching his arm as he passed him.

Dover glared at the cookhouse then dropped his hat back on his balding head. "I'm starving."

"Didn't you just eat?"

"If you want to call that eating," Dover returned, hitching his belt up over his protruding stomach. "Have to fill up on those lousy energy bars you got us a while back."

And before Cody could ask him more, Dover

was gone, his short, stubby legs pounding the dusty ground between the cookhouse and the bunkhouse.

Cody stepped into the cookhouse to the sound of grumbling and his heart dropped as a couple of the hands stared at him, looking as grumpy as Dover had.

Bryce sat at the table, frowning at his plate, Cade beside him poking something around on his plate. Even Ted, who had been so enthusiastic about hiring Vivienne, was looking at Bryce's food with a puzzled expression.

Not again, he thought with a feeling of inevitability.

He sent up another prayer for an extra dose of energy and pushed open the door to the kitchen.

Vivienne stood with her back to him, stirring something, her silly cook's hat crooked on her head.

Bowls, plates, pots and utensils covered every square inch of counter and even the butcher block table behind her. Even Stimpy Stevens, the cook who dipped a little too deeply into the cooking sherry, never made the kitchen this messy.

He was about to speak up when his little sister came out of the adjoining pantry carrying a bag of flour.

"Put the flour bag on the floor," Vivienne said.

"I'll take care of it. For now, bring those plates of food out to your uncle Ted and your brother."

As Bonnie set the flour down, Cody stifled a sigh. He thought her makeup was bad before. Today her lips were a bright crimson slash on a face adorned with pancake makeup. Her eyes were ringed with black and deep brown. She looked like a raccoon.

Obviously she had found the makeup he thought he had hidden.

"What in the world is going on here?" he called out, his voice coming out louder than he intended.

Vivienne spun around and her cheeks flamed red. Then she straightened, brushing her hands over her apron.

"Why are you here?" He pointed at Bonnie. "Why aren't you up at the house?"

Bonnie lifted her chin and Cody saw that defiant look take over her face as she grabbed a plate of food. "Vivienne needed help cooking and serving."

Which brought him to his original reason for coming here. Trouble was, he didn't know what to deal with first.

"Right now, Ms. Clayton and I need to talk and you need to go back to the house and wash your face."

Bonnie pressed her red lips together. "I'm not a little girl."

"Not the way you look," he concurred. He poked his thumb over his shoulder. "To the house. When I come back there, I want all that goop cleaned off your face."

She pursed her crimson lips and shot a quick glance at Vivienne, as if looking for help.

"Get your uncle Ted his dinner and dessert, and then you can go," Vivienne said quietly, and Bonnie left.

Which, in turn, made Cody feel as if he couldn't handle Bonnie on his own. Which made him feel even more frustrated. He knew he was being cranky and blamed it on a long day in the saddle and too many things weighing on his mind.

One of which was an uncle and partner spouting dumb ideas about the woman standing in front of him, her blond hair falling in loose wisps around her flushed face.

She looked as beautiful as she had in high school. More beautiful, if that was possible.

He shook his head to dislodge that thought. He had more important things to deal with.

When the kitchen door fell shut behind his little sister, he turned back to his cook. Belatedly he pulled his hat off and released his breath on a heavy sigh.

He couldn't help but be distracted by her looks. By her presence.

How was he supposed to do this?

Chapter Four

$\sim\!\!\sim$

The kitchen was a decent size, but somehow Cody's presence dominated the room. And as he glanced around at the pots, pans, dishes and bowls strewn over every available working space, she tried not to squirm.

Here it comes, Vivienne thought, a prickling dread working its way through her veins. Another failure.

"What is it?" Vivienne wiped her hands on her apron, then clasped them in front of her.

Cody gave her a curt nod of recognition as he slapped his hat against his leg. His blue jeans were coated in dust, as was his loose jacket, and his damp hair was plastered to his head. He looked rough and rugged.

And oddly appealing.

Vivienne wanted to give herself a shake. *You're about to lose a job, and you're making eyes at the man who's going to fire you?*

She straightened, determined to hold her head up in the face of whatever criticism was coming.

Cody scratched his one eyebrow with a forefinger and sighed. In that moment, Vivienne caught a look of utter weariness fall across his features. *He looks exhausted,* she thought with a flicker of compassion. Then his features tightened, his eyes narrowed and the moment fled.

"So what's for dinner?" he asked her.

"Cornish game hens and savory stuffing balls with chocolate mousse for dessert." Why had it sounded like such a good idea when she was making up the menu and so oddball now that she was saying it out loud to Cody?

Cody's frown told her exactly what he thought of that menu as he glanced around the kitchen. For a moment she saw it through his eyes. Saw the pots, pans, dishes and bowls spread over every available working space, and she struggled to stay composed.

"I usually keep my kitchen cleaner than this," she said, clenching her hands tighter to stop herself from fussing and tidying. "But I'm also used to having a couple of assistants."

"Is that why you got Bonnie to help?"

"She volunteered," Vivienne said in her defense, knowing exactly how Cody felt about Bonnie hanging around her.

"Stimpy didn't need help."

"And he was fired because he was careless," she retorted.

As were you.

She stifled the accusing thoughts. That was different.

Was it? Careless is careless.

"So why do you need help?"

She gestured around the kitchen. "I think this speaks for itself." She felt tired just looking at all the work ahead of her.

"I'm sure it would be easier if you made simpler food."

"Grilled cheese sandwiches is simple food." The retort came out before she could stop it. "I thought I would give the men something tasty."

"I don't know how tasty they thought it was," he said with a frown. "All I've heard was grumbling. Beans and biscuits would have been a better idea than what you dished up tonight."

Each word was like a blow to her own self-worth. Had she really lost her touch? Was she really such a failure as a chef that she couldn't even please cowboys?

"I said to keep it simple," Cody continued.

She rolled her eyes. "What I made wasn't that complicated."

"Savory stuffing balls for hungry hands? Seriously?"

Her cheeks tightened at his mockery. "Sorry,

I'll try to dumb down the menu." As soon as she spoke she realized how brusque that came out.

"It's just food, Miss Clayton," he retorted. "Fuel for the body."

All her training and years of work rebelled against this blunt comment. "Food is more than that. It's enjoyment. It's one of life's pleasures. It's…it's…" Her outrage at his ridiculous comment left her stumbling around trying to find how to explain how wrong he was.

"Food is calories," he said, cutting into her explanation. "Just make sure you give my men enough calories to do their job."

"Calories can still taste good." Vivienne tried to keep the prim note out of her voice but could tell from his raised eyebrow she hadn't succeeded. She realized she was butting against a brick wall. For now. "But I'll still need help even if I'm dumbing down the menu."

This netted her a heavy sigh. Cody ran his hand over his face and glanced around the cookhouse. "I can't spare any of the hands. I suppose I could talk to Delores, Grady's wife."

Grady, she understood, was one of the few married men who lived in a rented house on the ranch. "Delores has made it pretty clear she's not stepping foot in the kitchen again," Vivienne stated. "Which leaves me with Bonnie."

Cody's eyes narrowed. Why did it bother him so much?

"I know you don't like having Bonnie help," Vivienne continued, "but I also know she's bored...and bored teenage girls get into trouble. Especially when there's a couple of young men on the ranch."

Cody glared at her, but she could tell he was wavering.

"Bryce knows better than to get near my sister, and Cade is engaged to Jasmine Turner," he said.

"Cade Clayton is a grandson of Samuel Clayton," Vivienne said sharply. "I know my family thinks he's a good kid, but I don't know him well enough to form a positive opinion."

The history of the Claytons was checkered with double-dealings and backstabbings. A person didn't have to go too far into the family tree to find the source.

According to Cade's relatives, her grandfather, George Clayton, had swindled land and money and stolen the woman he'd loved from his brother, Samuel Clayton. Those half-truths and lies had been perpetuated by Samuel's children and grandchildren. As a result, Vivienne's side of the family, through George Senior, was hated by Samuel Clayton's side of the family.

One of whom was Cade. Cade's own cousins had been behind a string of problems that had dogged her family since Grandpa George's funeral and will. Had Cade been able to keep himself above the invective spoon-fed to each of his relatives on the Samuel Clayton side of the family? As she had told Cody, Brooke and Zach seemed to like Cade but she still struggled with who he was related to. Les, Vincent, Marsha and the rest never had anything good to say about Vivienne or her family members.

"You Claytons and your family feuds," Cody said in a voice that clearly expressed his opinion. "I don't care who did what when, but I trust Cade Clayton." Then he gave her a cool look she could only assume meant he didn't trust her. "And as for my sister, I'm not crazy about her working with you, but I agree that she needs to stay out of trouble." He shoved his hand through his hair. "She can help you in the kitchen once in a while and only when she doesn't have too much homework, but I want you to know I'll be watching you."

"Watching me for what?" Vivienne couldn't stop the words that burst out of her.

"Bonnie is easily influenced," Cody said, his voice growing grim. "And she wants like crazy to get away from the ranch. And I know you think Clayton is some hick town and you'll be leaving as soon as you can." He stopped there and then waved his hand between them as if to erase what he just said. "I'm sorry. That was uncalled for. What you do is none of my business."

Vivienne felt a confusing mixture of anger and shame at his comments. Yes, she was only staying around long enough for the money, and why shouldn't she? Clayton held nothing for her.

But at the same time, his opinion of her bothered her on a level she didn't want to examine too hard.

Then he looked around the kitchen again, shaking his head. "For now, I guess you'll have to clean this up yourself."

She wanted to make a comment but felt enough had been said for now. Tomorrow was another day.

"One more thing," he said, dropping his hat on his head. "In the next day or so I'd like to sit down with you and figure out a menu."

Her back stiffened at his suggestion. "I think I can figure things out for myself."

"Savory stuffing balls?"

"We covered that," Vivienne said, struggling to keep her wounded pride in check.

She had to believe the stuffing balls and the game hens were done to perfection. Considering what she had to work with, she thought she had done quite well. So what had gone so badly wrong that the men were so upset? Was she really as bad a cook as her former boss had accused her of being?

Her confidence wavered again, but she held his gaze. "I'll probably be up before you in the morning. What would you suggest I make for breakfast?"

"Bacon and eggs. Porridge. I don't care. Keep it simple and keep it edible."

There went her plan of Belgian buttermilk waffles with glazed bananas. "Okay. You're the boss."

"Just remember that," Cody shot back. Then he shook his head and turned to leave.

"You didn't get your dinner," she called out, picking up the plate of food she had made up. She wanted him to see for himself what the men had been complaining about. Wanted to find out from him what he thought.

He glanced down at the proffered plate. "Sorry. I'm not hungry."

Don't take it personally, she reminded herself as she turned away from him. *Maybe he's really not hungry.*

But she couldn't help feeling that when he rejected her food, he was rejecting her.

Why do you care? After all...he's a cowboy. You're a city girl.

Yet, as he left, Vivienne felt as if some vitality and energy had left the room with him.

She brushed the silly feeling aside and turned

back to the dirty pots and pans and dishes. She would be here until midnight cleaning up from a meal no one seemed to like. That was enough to make even the most experienced chef depressed.

The next morning Cody stepped inside the cookhouse, his stomach growling so loud he was surprised it didn't drown out the complaining he heard rumbling through the building. After he left the cookhouse last night, he'd gone straight to his own house. Bonnie was hiding out in her bedroom. So he satisfied himself with a meal of cold cereal while he paid the bills and balanced the checkbook.

As a result, this morning, he was starving. But the sound of the griping going on in the cookhouse this morning made him want to pull his hat over his head and turn and leave.

Then Dover stood up, his back to Cody, and looked around at the gathered men, his meaty hands on his hips. "Okay, so we drew straws to see who goes to talk to her. Cade, you drew short straw, so it's your job."

"Give me a break, guys." Cade Clayton held up his hands in a gesture of surrender. "I don't want her mad at me."

"C'mon. Young buck like you. Those shoulders. That Clayton blond hair," Bryce teased, giving Cade's belly a poke. "Rock-hard abs. What's to be mad about? Besides, she's your third or fourth cousin or something like that."

Cade gave him a wry look. "Second cousin. And on the other branch of the family tree."

"What's going on?" Cody asked, hanging his jacket on the peg inside the door. As he walked across the wooden floor, his spurs jangled in the quiet.

"Cade drew short straw. He's gotta talk to his cousin Vivienne about her cooking," Dover said, scratching his ample belly. "'Cause I tell you, what's happened the last two meals isn't workin' for us."

Cody angled his chin toward the empty bowls scattered over the table. "What was for breakfast?"

"Some kind of bread pudding," Bryce put in.

Cody groaned. What happened to the bacon and eggs he suggested?

"Why don't you talk to her," Ted suggested. "She'll listen to you." His uncle lifted his eyebrows in a suggestive manner that made Cody clench his jaw.

"Why do I have to go? You're as much a partner as I am," Cody said to his uncle Ted.

Ted shrugged and then winked. "Your shoulders got way more pull than mine."

Cody nailed his uncle with a sharp look, but Ted wasn't fazed.

"I don't have time for this malarkey," Cody grumbled even as he marched to the kitchen door and shoved it open. Why couldn't he get anyone on this place to listen to him?

Vivienne stood by the sink, her hair pulled up, looking a lot less flushed than she did yesterday. She hummed a quiet tune, looking content and pleased with herself.

Gold hoops dangled from her ears and she wore a silk scarf around her neck. Like she was all dressed up for something. Or someone. Then she turned and the smile on her face went straight to his gut.

"Good morning, Cody. Is Bonnie coming to help me?" She angled her head to one side and gently brushed a strand of hair back from her face.

"No."

Vivienne blew out her breath. "I thought—"

Cody held up his hand. One problem at a time. "She's finishing up homework she sloughed off last night. She has to get it done before the bus comes to get her."

"I see. Did you both have your breakfast?"

He shook his head. "Bonnie doesn't eat breakfast."

"What?" Vivienne looked horrified. "It's the most important meal of the day."

Hearing her parrot the same words his mom

had always said to him gave him a momentary feeling of nostalgia. He waved off her comment.

"Maybe, but I'm not getting into that fight with her," he said. He had to save his ammunition for bigger battles. Like trying to find a way to spend quality time with his sister, getting his work done and keeping her away from the single cowboys on this ranch.

Once again he wished his parents had sent his sister somewhere else. He didn't have time to take care of her properly.

"Did *you* have breakfast?" Vivienne asked.

"Just got here in time to hear the men grumbling. Again. About the food you made."

Her smile dropped away into a frown and he felt like smacking himself on the head. That came out all wrong, but something about her tangled his thoughts, which plugged up his conversational filter.

"What could the men possibly be groping about now?" she said. "I made a simple breakfast, like you told me. Bread pudding, of all things." She balled her hands into fists and dropped them onto her hips. "Those ungrateful louses. I spent a lot of time on that breakfast."

"From the sounds of their grumbling, you might have been better off with porridge packs."

"Porridge packs? What are you talking about?" Cody shook his head, trying to comprehend the fact that this fancy, New York chef didn't understand one of the staples of breakfast out on the trail. "You boil the water. You rip open the porridge packet. You put the two together in a bowl. Stir and eat."

Vivienne made a face as if he had suggested she use mud. "You can't be serious. I actually know which ingredients go into the food I cook. None of that butylated hydroxytoluene added to packaging material to preserve freshness."

"What?"

"Never mind." Vivienne held up her hand. "Work joke."

"What I am serious about is you doing what I ask. You've cooked two meals for my guys, and both times they've bombed. Even old Stimpy Stevens didn't have that bad a track record."

Vivienne pulled back as if he had hit her. "But…I…" She pressed her lips together and turned away.

"I want you to make up a menu and bring it over tomorrow. That way we can figure out what you can make that would keep my hands happy."

Then the door opened behind him.

"Did you tell her, boss?" Dover said in a stage whisper.

Cody shot a look over his shoulder. All he saw of Dover was his head poking through the door, his grizzled cheeks glinting in the light from the kitchen. Then, another head appeared above him. Grady. "Did you ask her if there's more?" Grady asked, also whispering.

"More? What are you talking about?" Cody asked, genuinely puzzled.

The door opened farther and Cody could see the men gathered behind Dover and Grady, their hats in their hands. They looked like a bunch of schoolboys with a crush on their teacher.

"What is going on?" Cody's gaze flicked from his men, then back to Vivienne, who looked as befuddled as he was.

Then Cade lurched forward, as if pushed.

"Can I help you, Cade?" Vivienne asked, bracing herself for more criticism.

Cade shot Cody a pleading look, then cleared his throat in a nervous gesture. "The guys asked me to talk to you about the food. About you making more."

Cody and Vivienne spoke at the same time. "What?"

"Yeah. It was great. I've never tasted bread pudding that was so good," Cade was saying. "But there wasn't enough. I really wanted seconds, but there wasn't any left over."

"I wanted seconds, too," Dover put in.

"What you wanted was thirds," Grady said, giving him a light shove.

Dover shrugged, then licked his lips as if remembering that second helping of breakfast.

"So that was the only problem this morning?" Vivienne asked.

They all nodded.

"Was that also what you characters were belly-aching about last night?" Cody asked.

"Our bellies ached all right," Dover said, rubbing his ample stomach. "Only 'cause they were still empty. I could have eaten a dozen of those round things. What were they?"

"Savory stuffing balls." Again Cody and Vivienne spoke at the same time.

Cody shook his head as if trying to settle his confusion. He thought the guys were griping about the cooking, but instead their biggest complaint was how much she had made?

"Supper was great, Vivienne," his uncle Ted said, moving into the kitchen. "But we came back from a long, hard day of work. Those little hens and those few ball things just didn't do the job. And the pudding this morning… I never thought you could make plain ordinary bread taste so good." He sighed. "But again, not enough to hold these guys for a long day in the saddle. Especially when all they get for lunch is energy bars." Ted angled Cody a sharp look.

Cody ignored his uncle the same way as he'd been ignored a few moments ago, then he glanced at Vivienne beside him, her carefully manicured fingers pressed to her lips.

"You guys like the food," she said, as if she didn't believe it herself.

"Yeah. It's great, just not enough."

She released a relieved laugh. "I apologize," she said quietly. "I'm so accustomed to New York portions. I can definitely increase the quantity if that's the only difficulty."

"Is there any more of that bread stuff?" Bryce asked, stepping forward, holding his trucker cap in both hands. "We're all still hungry."

Vivienne glanced at Cody. "If you can spare your men for another half an hour, I can make some more."

Cody bit his lip, debating. "I wanted to be up in the hills before the cattle start moving around too much. And the horses need to be saddled up. Can't you just give them toast?"

The collective groan from the men told him that toast wouldn't cut it. And he knew if he didn't give in on this the day ahead would be one long whine-fest.

One of these days they had to have a meeting about who was the boss around here. He turned back to Vivienne. "So, you can make more of that bread pudding quick enough to feed these men of mine and get us on our way before the cows decide to head over the pass?" He tossed a quick glare over his shoulder to remind the men of the real reason they were here. To work.

"I can, but I can have it done faster if I have help," Vivienne said with a shrug.

And Bonnie was heading out for school in twenty minutes.

His uncle Ted stepped forward, hitching up his pants. "You stay here and help Vivienne, Cody. I'll take the men out and get the horses ready. They can be tied up while we eat and then we'll be out the door with hardly any time wasted."

And before Cody could protest this plan, Uncle Ted herded the men out the door with promises of more food when they came back.

Cody watched them go, stifling his irritation with his uncle. Why did he have the feeling he'd been railroaded?

Chapter Five

❧

"You don't have to peel the apples, just cut them. Like this." Vivienne took a knife she had recently sharpened and demonstrated. The knife flashed and in a few seconds a pile of cut-up pieces of apple lay on the cutting board.

"I can't do it that fast," Cody protested, taking the knife from her.

As they did, their hands brushed, and Vivienne had to force herself not to yank her hand back. *No unexpected movements around sharp knives,* she could hear her cooking instructor say.

"You only need to cut up a few apples," Vivienne said, puzzled at the breathless note in her voice. She wasn't sure why, but she felt fully aware of every move Cody made. His height. The breadth of his shoulders.

The way his mouth puckered up when he was thinking.

She had wanted to protest when Ted had made

his plan, but some strange part of her didn't mind having Cody Jameson in her kitchen, standing beside her.

She measured out the milk, frowning at the amount she had left. "I'll need to get more groceries if I'm cooking larger quantities of food."

"That's okay."

"Trouble is, my car badly needs an oil change, and there's something wrong with the brakes."

She really needed a new car, but that would have to wait. For now, as long as this car could be doctored, she could limp along with it for the next while.

"Bring it to Art's," Cody said. "I'm headed to that part of town in a couple of days, and I can take you back if the car isn't done on time."

"Okay." She beat some more eggs and added the milk, trying to stifle her awareness of Cody standing beside her, still patiently cutting the apples.

"Just a question," she asked. "How do I pay for the groceries?"

Cody shot her a frown. "How did you pay for the food you bought before?"

"I put it on my credit card."

"Let me know how much it was and I'll pay you back." Cody handed her the cutting board with the apples on it. "Do you have the bills yet?"

"I threw them away. I suppose you'd need the bills for tax purposes."

"Pretty much."

"Then just leave it. Chalk it up to a lesson learned," she said, adding spices to the milk-and-egg mixture. "When I own my restaurant, I'll have to be more businesslike."

"That what you want to do with the money from your grandpa George?" Cody asked, rinsing off the knife and dropping it in the knife block.

Vivienne nodded, her lips curving up in a smile as her mind easily slipped back to her plans and dreams. "It's what I wanted to do since I graduated from Le Cordon Bleu in Paris."

"What kind of restaurant would you run, and… what else do you want me to do?"

"Can you cut the crusts of the bread off and then slice it into cubes?" She pointed to the loaf on the counter. "As for the restaurant, I don't have a vision or theme yet, other than fine dining."

"So, no grilled cheese sandwiches on your menu?" Cody said, snagging the plastic bag holding the bread.

Vivienne smiled at his attempt at a joke, recognizing it as a small olive branch. "If there were, they'd be gourmet grilled cheese sandwiches. With dill sauce and roasted red peppers and caciocavallo podolico cheese."

"I'm guessing that's not cheddar," Cody said,

giving her a quick grin as he ripped open the bread bag.

His smile distracted her from his ruining a perfectly good plastic bag. "It's Italian," Vivienne replied. "Made from the milk of free-range cows. And it costs five hundred dollars a pound."

"I'd suggest leaving that off the menu." Cody grabbed another knife from the block and started cutting. Vivienne added a few more spices to the egg mixture and turned the oven on. She got out another baking pan for the bread pudding and greased it up with butter. The kitchen was well stocked with pans, bowls and containers.

"What can I do now?" Cody asked when he was finished.

"Just give me the bread and I'll soak it in the egg mixture and then grate cinnamon over top."

She reached for the bowl and endured a moment of awkwardness as he handed it to her. Once again she caught herself far too aware of him.

As she mixed the bread cubes into the milk mixture she shook her reaction off, blaming it on her lonely single state.

During her focused climb up the career ladder, she had a few boyfriends, and the one guy she'd become serious about had dumped her. So she maintained her focus, her mother's mantra pounding in her head.

Take care of yourself, because no man will.

So she had. But all that taking care of herself had come at a cost. And where had all that self-discipline gotten her?

Stuck out on a ranch, making gourmet bread pudding, hoping and, yes, praying her cousins Mei and Lucas would come home, as well, to fulfill the terms of Grandpa George's will. If they didn't all come, this work and sacrifice was for nothing.

And even if she did get the money and could start up a restaurant, then what? Go back to New York. Start the restaurant. Alone.

Vivienne yanked a cinnamon stick out of the jar and grated it over the pudding, her movements quick and harsh. *Shouldn't matter. Take care of yourself.*

"Slow down there," Cody warned, frowning at her. "You don't want to hurt yourself."

"I'm fine," she said, her fears and frustrations spilling out into her actions. Then her finger slipped and her knuckles slammed against the grater, the force of her movement slashing the skin off two knuckles.

She sucked in a breath and pulled her hand close to her.

"Careful," Cody said, grabbing her hand and holding it away from her as blood streamed down her fingers onto the cuff of her sweater. He pulled her along behind him. "Come over to the sink."

He turned on the tap and pulled her hand underneath the stream of water. The cold water stung, and Vivienne winced as he carefully washed the blood away. "Do you know where the first-aid kit is?" he asked.

She shook her head, biting her lip against the burning pain, watching the water running over her finger.

"Just stay here. I'll be right back." Cody spun away.

She was about to pull her hand away from the water when he returned with the first-aid kit. "Found it," he said, setting the tin on the butcher-block counter beside her. He turned the water off and caught her hand once again, his callused fingers rough against her skin.

"It's okay," she said, tugging her hand back. "I can take care of this."

"Not really," he muttered, dabbing at her knuckles with a clean towel. "Hold still and I'll get this bandaged up." He whistled as the blood kept flowing. "You really did a number on those knuckles," he said, opening up the emergency kit with one hand. "Press this against your fingers while I try to get these bandage packages open."

Vivienne did as he said, hot flashes of pain stabbing her hand. "I feel like such a sissy," she said, wincing. "It's just a flesh wound."

"Those hurt the most," he said as he ripped

open a package of gauze. "All your nerves are just below the surface of your skin, so you feel every scrape." He took her hand once again, his movements gentle as he peeled away the now-red towel. Then he bent over her, his head so close to hers she could see the wave in his hair, the fine lines fanning away from his eyes, white from squinting against the sun all summer.

Though it was already October, his skin was still tanned and dark. A man of the outdoors, she thought, watching as his large hands deftly wound the bandages around her finger.

Their eyes met, and as the moment lengthened Vivienne felt as if time slipped backward.

Once again they were two teenagers standing on the parking lot as a question hovered between them. *Would she?*

What would her life have been like if she had said yes to him all those years ago? Would she be feeling as empty as she felt now in spite of all her accomplishments? Her supposed drive to be the best chef she could be?

Or would she have sold herself short, dating a cowboy? Missing out on opportunities?

She saw his Adam's apple bob as he swallowed and she wondered if he was as affected by her as she was by him.

"I don't think you'll need stitches," he said, his voice gruff.

"But will I be able to play the violin?" she asked, grabbing for an old, tired joke to diffuse the situation.

He cleared his throat and wrapped some tape around her fingers. "Not right away, but maybe once your fingers heal."

"That's great, because I never could before."

Cody gave her a wry look. "Walked right into that one," he said.

"I've always wanted to use that but never had a chance."

He pressed down the last bit of tape and finally released her hand. "Glad I could be your straight man." He stepped back as if creating a distance for himself, as well. "High school all over again."

She frowned at the reference. "What do you mean by that?"

He shrugged, giving her a wry grin. "I know I was just a joke to you then."

"No…you weren't."

Cody released a light laugh. "C'mon, Vivienne. You were a Clayton. So much a part of the history of the town you had the same name. Me? I was just a Jameson. Parents always gone. Always barely getting by financially."

Vivienne cradled her throbbing hand in her other hand. "What makes you think my life was so different from yours just because I had a history in this town? My father died when I was a teenager, and my mother never got past that. We always just got by, as well."

"But your grandfather—"

"Never gave us a red cent." She couldn't stop the burst of anger accompanying those words. "Why do you think he's giving us this money now that he's gone? Because he felt guilty about how he treated the people in his life—his own family—right up until the end. As far as I can see, this inheritance is too little, too late."

"I wouldn't call a quarter of a million dollars and five hundred acres of deeded land too little," Cody said as he cleaned up the papers from the bandaids.

Vivienne realized how petty she sounded. "It is a lot of money. And don't think I'm not appreciative. But even in spite of his generosity, he still has to be the one with the final say. Still has to manipulate even from the grave."

"What do you mean?"

"I'll only get the money if all the cousins come home by Christmas and everyone sticks around for a year. So far, Brooke, Zach and Arabella seem to be settled enough. But Mei and Lucas are the wild cards. They don't show up, none of us get any of it." Vivienne pushed back a quiver of fear at the thought that Mei, who so often felt as if she wasn't a part of this family, and Lucas, who had always gone his own way, wouldn't be there. "They don't show up and stick around, then I've just wasted a year hanging around here."

"Is that what you think staying around Clayton would be? A waste?"

As he spoke, Vivienne felt the old fear rise up. Fear of staying in Clayton, stuck in the endless rut of barely getting by. Always wondering if something better was happening somewhere else. Something more exciting, more interesting.

"This town is dying, Cody," she said quietly. "I don't see a lot of future for it."

"Your money could help," he replied.

"How?"

"The town needs new businesses, new capital injected into it. We could use a decent store. We get tourists coming through, but they never stop. Nothing to stop for."

Vivienne felt a tiny glimmer as he spoke, thinking of possibilities. But she shook them off. She had her plans and she had to stick with them.

"I can't see that anything I could do could help this town. I've had goals and dreams ever since I left this place that I have invested time and money into."

"So there's no way you'd stick around here." Cody's comment came out as more of a statement than a question, but as their eyes met, she felt it again. That glimmer of attraction hearkening back to older emotions and a younger self.

The moment lingered. She wanted to look away and break a connection that could create problems for her. This was not in her plans.

She tore her gaze away from his and, turning away from him, ignored the throbbing in her hands and finished putting the bread pudding together, then she set it in the oven. "Clayton only holds bad memories for me. Even if I don't get the money, I'm out of here as soon as possible."

The silence following her pronouncement held weight, and for a moment she regretted being so blunt.

But it was the truth, and if she wanted to keep her eye on the prize, she knew she had to stick with the plan no matter what.

Cody took a breath, as if he was about to say something, then he turned and left. As the door fell shut behind him Vivienne felt as if some life force had gone with him.

She shook it off and, ignoring the stinging in her fingers, started cleaning up the kitchen. It shouldn't matter to her what he thought of her.

But somehow, even as she tried to convince herself of that, another tiny voice told her she was lying.

"So I hear Vivienne's cooking for you now." Billy Dean Harris wiped the grease off his hands as he and Cody walked toward the front of Art

Krueger's mechanic shop. Billy worked at the shop when he felt like it, and when he needed ready cash. "Bet that's kind of handy for you. What with the way you used to like her and all," he said with a broad wink.

"That was a long time ago," Cody said.

"Yeah, and oh, of course, you were married before." Billy shoved the towel in the back pocket of stained overalls straining against his protruding stomach. Then he pulled the keys off a large board with hooks that held the key rings of the other vehicles awaiting service at the shop. "Though it was a shame about Tabitha. Guess she wasn't cut out for ranch living. Not many women are. You want a coffee?" Cody glanced at the dusty coffeemaker perched on a sagging shelf below the keyboard, mugs set upside down beside it. "No, thanks."

Billy Dean dropped Cody's keys on the counter and then rested his elbows there, as if settling in for a chat. "My Marsha could never live out on the ranch. 'Course, Marsha was as amazed as I was to hear that uppity Vivienne could. Girl was always too fancy for her blue jeans. I'm surprised she's willin' to lower herself to cook on a ranch for a bunch of cowboys."

"She needs the work," Cody said, picking up the keys as he took a step away from the desk. He hoped Billy would get the hint. He had to go to the bank yet, meet Vivienne at the grocery store, then pick up his sister from school.

"Yeah, I hear she's only stickin' 'round long enough to get her paws on that money from her louse of a grandfather," Billy Dean said, a sneer curling his lip. "Vivienne Clayton's only got one thing on her mind—her grandpa George's money—and what she's gotta do to get her hands on it. Too bad there's so many hoops those cousins got to jump through before they get it." Billy gave Cody a quick grin. "A year is a long time. Lots could happen between now and then."

Billy's words came too close to his own feelings about Vivienne. "Thanks for doing the oil change on the truck on such short notice," he said, ending the conversation.

"Tell Vivienne that her car won't be ready tomorrow like we figgered. Boss needs to order in brake pads, and there's been trouble with her brake lines and her tranny. Trouble is, she told us not to get new parts, so we're scrounging around for a used one. The soonest we can get 'er done is couple of days." Billy Dean pushed himself away from the counter. "And tell Bryce that I need to talk to him next time he has a chance to come to town."

"I'll pass the messages on."

"And you make sure that Vivienne girl don't

get you wrapped around her little finger like she used to brag about when you was in high school."

Cody wished he could ignore the snide words, but they slithered too close to his own insecurities when it came to Vivienne. Had she really thought that? Said that?

Forget it. That was then. This is now. He tossed off a wave and walked out of the shop.

He tried not to let Billy's comments bother him as he drove away, but at the same time he knew Billy Dean was only speaking a truth Cody knew as clearly as anyone. Vivienne Clayton had told him herself. She was only staying around until she could collect the money.

Why did that bother him? She meant nothing to him. Yet he knew part of him had never completely forgotten Vivienne.

She's a city girl, Cody reminded himself as he drove toward the grocery store. Tabitha was a city girl.

The thought of his wife made his gut twist with regret, pain and anger. Tabitha was a mistake he had no intention of repeating. Tabitha brought him nothing but pain and heartbreak.

He best remember that if he was having any foolish notions about one Miss Vivienne Clayton.

Because she was, in so many ways, exactly like his wife.

* * *

"Sure you can't stay longer?" Brooke asked, her voice filled with regret.

Vivienne finished the last of her lemonade and set the glass on the tray on the table in front of the porch swing. The wooden swing hanging from chains attached to the verandah's ceiling was a new addition to the family home. Brooke's fiancé had installed it when Brooke had casually mentioned to him that she would love a porch swing. A few days later, there it hung. "I only have ten more minutes." She also wished she didn't have to rush away. It had been years since she'd been able to talk face-to-face with Brooke instead of over the phone or via e-mail. But duty called. "Cody is taking the groceries back to the ranch in his truck, and I want to go over the order with Les before he takes it away."

Brooke pushed the swing with her toe, the chain squeaking just like it used to when they were little.

Memories flooded Vivienne as she glanced over the front lawn, now strewn with blocks and pails. Detritus from A.J. playing on the lawn until Brooke took him upstairs for a nap.

Lucy used to play on the lawn, too, Vivienne thought. The memory of their little sister, now passed away, created a soft ache deep in her heart. She hadn't thought of Lucy since she left Clayton.

"I think your boss would forgive you if you batted your eyes harder and did that famous Vivienne hair toss," Brooke said, pushing the swing again. "Plus, you have that sore finger. Could always use that."

Vivienne rolled her own eyes. "Cody Jameson wouldn't notice the hair toss, especially because I usually keep it tied up in a ponytail." She glanced at the bandage on her finger, remembering that moment in the kitchen yesterday. When he bandaged it. When their faces were almost touching. "And I'm sure he hasn't given my sore finger a second thought," she added. "That man does nothing but work. I feel like something is bothering him."

"He did lose his wife."

Vivienne nodded, seeing once again the lines of weariness edging Cody's mouth. He looked as if he was grieving a loss of some kind. "I think it's more than that, but he'll never tell me."

Vivienne was about to say something more when a small car parked in front of Brooke's house. "Are you expecting company?"

"Darlene asked if she could stop by with Macy," Brooke said, getting to her feet and brushing the crumbs of the cookies off her khaki pants.

Darlene Perry got out of the car and leaned an arm on its roof. Her hair hung lanky down her back, and Vivienne could see that, in spite of her illness, at one time she had been a beauty.

"She looks so frail." Vivienne spoke quietly, concerned. "Should she still be driving?"

"Zach says she's fine to drive once in a while," Brooke said as the other car door opened. Darlene's daughter Macy bailed out of the car, her blond hair streaming behind her as she ran up the walk toward Brooke. The little girl's vitality was a stark contrast to her mother, who was slowly making her way around the front of the car.

Brooke had told Vivienne about Darlene. How she was dying and concerned about leaving her daughter Macy behind with no family. Darlene had reached out to members of their family, asking them to be involved in Macy's life. Vivienne felt sorry for Darlene, who as far as Vivienne knew, had no relatives in Clayton. Leaving Macy without family must be an ache in Darlene's heart, Vivienne thought. Though she wondered why Darlene had singled out their family to connect with.

Brooke caught the little girl in a hug, and as she pulled away, Macy pushed her pink glasses back up her nose. "How was school today, Macy?" Brooke asked, kneeling down and getting on the little girl's level.

Macy's only reply was a shrug, looking past Brooke to Vivienne. "Who's that lady?" she asked, pointing.

Darlene had caught up to Brooke and Macy by then and gently pushed her daughter's hand down. "It's rude to point, honey," she said quietly.

"But who is she?" Macy pressed.

"My name is Vivienne. I'm Brooke's sister." Vivienne came down the walk to meet them both.

Darlene brightened at that. "You're the one who cooks?"

"I'm a trained gourmet chef, yes," Vivienne said.

"I like to cook," Macy piped up. "I can make hot chocolate and porridge. I just have to boil water."

Vivienne smiled, thinking of Cody's comment yesterday morning. It seemed instant porridge was a major food group in Clayton. "That's a good start," Vivienne said.

"I've always wanted to cook," Darlene said, glancing down at her daughter. "But I'm not very good at it. I would love to be able to teach Macy, but I'm afraid that's not happening."

Brooke clapped her hands as if to dispel the sadness of the moment. "I have the best idea, Vivienne. Why don't you hold a cooking class? On the ranch? I know I'd come. And Macy could come. And Jasmine. Arabella said Jasmine wants to take culinary classes when she and Cade move away after the wedding. This would be a great chance for her to try it out."

Vivienne tried to imagine what Cody would think of this horde of women descending on his ranch. "I just started there. I'm not sure my boss would appreciate it." But even as she spoke, she glanced at Macy, who was looking at her with wide eyes, a dimple teasing one cheek.

"I'd love to learn to cook," she said, a note of yearning in her voice.

And that sealed the deal. Vivienne would find a way to make this happen. With children who were hurting, there was an unspoken rule that if it was possible to grant a wish, an adult had the responsibility to do so.

"Okay. I'll talk to Cody," she said, "But don't expect too much," she said. A quick glance at her watch made her jump. "I gotta get going," she said. She gave Brooke a quick hug, tossed off a wave to Darlene and then slung her purse over her shoulder.

She strode down the street she had been born and raised on, the chill in the air reminding her that winter was coming and coming soon.

She breathed in the fresh air of moldering leaves and damp dirt as she hurried across the street, then skirted the park. Leaves fluttered down as she walked, old memories mingling with the present. How often had she, Brooke and Zach run down this street, heading toward school, coats wide open, scarves trailing behind them as their mother called out from the porch to zip up their coats. Life had been hard after their father died. But she and her family still had good times, as well.

She let the memories surface. She remembered a few random visits from her grandfather. The occasional gift he'd send their way.

Now, if everything went well, she would receive a whole lot more than just miniature cake pans she could bake with. She would get a chance at a new life. At starting her own restaurant. Controlling her own life as her mother had always pushed her to.

A car honked as it passed her and Vivienne waved, recognizing an old school friend. As she walked past the Cowboy Café, Kylie knocked on the window and waggled her fingers at her.

The grocery store, just across Barn Owl Road, was busy when she got there. When she stepped inside, the ringing of the cash register mingled with the voices of people chatting as they waited to be served. It sounded like home, she thought, glancing around the bright interior of the grocery store.

A young woman, pushing a grocery cart laden with plastic bags and holding a toddler on her hip, shot her a smile and greeted her by name as she passed her. Vivienne was sure she knew her, but she couldn't pull a name out fast enough.

For a moment, Vivienne was glad to be back in Clayton. Back to a place where everybody knew you and knew your name. Where people really cared about each other. New York City had an energy, an excitement, but she hadn't found community there like she had here growing up.

"So, one by one the Clayton kiddies are coming home to roost."

The raspy voice of her aunt Katrina broke into Vivienne's thoughts, and as she turned, Vivienne caught a strong whiff of cigarette smoke emanating from her aunt's jacket.

Aunt Katrina stood beside her, an empty grocery basket hanging from one thin arm, her red hair sticking out in sharp spikes. She wore a pink silky jacket over a black lace shirt and purple leggings that did nothing for her knobby knees. Her green eyes glanced up and down at Vivienne's dress, then gave her niece a broad smile. "New York's been ever so good to you, honey. You look like a million dollars." Then she laughed. "Or should I say a quarter of a million?"

"Hello, Aunt Katrina," Vivienne said, not sure if she should give Arabella's mother a hug or simply smile. Vivienne had never been particularly close to Aunt Kat, but she had a few good memories of visiting Arabella's house before Arabella's father and Aunty Kat got divorced. "Nice to see you again."

"Yeah. I'm sure it is." Aunt Kat patted her lightly on the shoulder, her long earrings jangling as she did so. "Hear you're stuck at the ranch."

"I'm cooking there, yes."

"If you see that little weasel, Bryce, tell him I need to talk to him."

Vivienne frowned at that. She didn't know Aunt Kat and Bryce knew each other, but then Clayton was a small town. Everyone knew everyone in one way or another. "I'll tell him next time I see him."

"Please do that." Aunt Kat released a harsh laugh. "And enjoy your time at the ranch. Good thing it's only temporary. Soon enough you'll get your money and you can be gone." She added a wink, then strolled past Vivienne, wafting stale cigarette smoke behind her.

Then Vivienne turned and almost bumped into Cody. She glanced up and, to her dismay, felt again that peculiar lift of her heart as their eyes met.

"You ready to go?" he asked, his voice gruff.

"I just have to find Les and check over the order he put together for me. Make sure he put everything in I asked for."

"I'm sure you can trust him, even though he's

one of the 'evil' Claytons," Cody said, his voice holding a sarcastic edge. "We already loaded it all in the truck. Sorry, but I gotta pick up Bonnie from school, and I want to be back at the ranch on time."

Vivienne hesitated, torn between a need to make sure she had all the supplies she needed and knowing that Cody had his own schedule to keep. Whenever she took a delivery at the restaurant, she always went over it before the delivery van left, making sure everything they ordered was there. She knew once she got out to the ranch that if something was missing, she would have to make do until they went to the market again.

She curbed her need to control the situation. "Can we stop by and pick up my car?"

"Billy Dean said it won't be ready for at least a week. He had to get some parts from an auto wrecker, and it might take extra time. So you'll have to ride back to the ranch with me."

Vivienne wasn't sure she wanted to do that, but it seemed she had no choice. So she followed Cody as he strode to the door, yanked it open, then stepped aside.

The little courtesy was probably second nature to him, and she doubted that he was even aware he did it. And then, when he sauntered ahead of her and opened the truck door for her, as well, his courteous actions created a shimmer of warmth.

She was an independent woman of the twenty-first century. Such actions belonged to another time and place. Or so she had been told by her friends in New York.

Yet, in spite of being a modern woman, it felt good to be taken care of. And as they drove away from the store, she couldn't help the occasional surreptitious glance Cody's way.

He drove with one hand on the steering wheel, the other resting on the armrest of his door. A frown pulled his dark eyebrows together, as if he were already thinking about the work that lay ahead. She didn't know if she was being hypersensitive, but it was as if a tension had filled the truck. Thankfully it was only a short drive to the high school.

Bonnie stood with a group of friends when they pulled up to the high school parking lot. As Cody got out and walked toward his sister, Vivienne's mind trailed back to another time and almost exactly the same place.

She studied Cody from the safety of the truck. Watched as he lightly touched his sister on the shoulder, felt her heart warm at the gentle smile on his face. He really loved Bonnie. The same way she knew Zach cared about her and about Brooke.

But Bonnie shrugged his hand away, and from her vantage point, Vivienne easily caught the eye roll and curled lip Bonnie sent her friends. Vivienne wanted to give the ungrateful girl a shake.

Yet, even as she critiqued the young girl's behavior, Vivienne wondered what kind of expression she had on her face after she turned away from Cody Jameson. After she had turned him down. What feelings had she telegraphed to her friends?

She'd had no right to treat him so shamefully. Her age, at that time, was no excuse. Her mother had taught her better than that. She wished she could go back in time. Redo the moment.

And what do you think would have happened then?

She pushed the question aside. It didn't matter. She'd been wrong to treat him the way she had.

Bonnie slung her knapsack over her shoulder and handed Cody her jacket, like he was her personal valet. And in spite of her own degrading memories, or maybe because of them, Vivienne promised, first chance she had, she would let Bonnie know how disrespectful her behavior to her brother was.

As Bonnie came near the truck, Vivienne got out to let her in, but Bonnie held back. "I don't want to sit in the middle," she said, pouting.

"You can there or you sit in the box with the groceries," Cody replied, getting into the truck.

Bonnie stood by the open door, her bright red

lips clamped together, her expression mutinous. "I want to sit by the window. I get car sick if I sit in the middle."

"Missie, get in the truck. Now. I don't have time for this."

Vivienne glanced from Bonnie to Cody as the tension mounted. She guessed Bonnie wasn't giving in. Yet if she sat in the middle, that would put her right up beside Cody.

Not preferable.

"Then I'll walk home." Bonnie tossed her hair and was about to turn to leave when Vivienne caught her by the arm.

"Don't be silly," she reprimanded. "I'll sit in the middle."

She tried not to let the girl's triumphant look get to her as she climbed in. Because once Cody drove away, she had other things to keep her occupied.

Like how she could keep her distance when every corner he turned brought the two of them in close contact.

She kept her eyes on the road, but it was as if every nerve of her being was aware of Cody beside her. She could smell the scent of his aftershave, could feel the warmth of his arm as it brushed hers when he shifted.

Keep your eye on the prize, she thought, staring

out the window as they drove out of town. *Don't think about the man sitting beside you. Don't let yourself be distracted.*

Chapter Six

"Did you check all your work?" Cody dragged his hand over his face, then pulled his chair closer to the kitchen table and picked up the math textbook again.

He was helping Bonnie with her homework. It had been years since he'd done this, and his own calculations were rusty. As a result, things were not going well.

Bonnie tossed her pencil down on the table. "Of course I did. And the answer is still wrong." She dropped her arms over her chest in a gesture of anger and defiance. "I hate math. I hate school and I hate being stuck out here on the ranch."

Cody winged up yet another hasty prayer as he repressed his frustration. Why did the women in his life hate living out on the ranch so much? "But it's so peaceful here," he said, trying to show her the positives. "It's quiet and you can think out here. You can go out for a walk anytime you want. I always feel freer out here."

You're feeling freer right about now?

He pushed the traitorous question aside. Sure he was having his struggles right now, but in time it would all resolve itself. In time he would forget about Tabitha's betrayal. In time his life would fall into some kind of rhythm.

And he'd get used to being alone.

"You know you're only staying on the ranch until mom and dad come back," he told his sister, hoping to reassure her. "I lived out here, too, whenever they would leave."

Bonnie pressed her lips together as if angry, but not before Cody caught a telltale quiver and his anger melted away.

"Hey, Bonnie, they said they're calling tomorrow." He remembered the times he would stay out on the ranch, as well. Bonnie was young back then, and being on the ranch was still an adventure for her. She used to love picking wildflowers, feeding carrots to the horses and going for aimless walks. How things changed.

"As if that will help," she groused. "I'm still stuck out here."

A knock on the door saved him from his sister's melodrama. Probably Ted coming to go over the plans for the next week.

"Come in," he called out, picking up the pencil Bonnie had tossed on the table.

"Sorry to bother you…"

Cody dropped the pencil and spun around. The quiet voice was definitely not his uncle's.

Vivienne stood in the doorway of the kitchen, holding a folder. The glimmer of dangly earrings in her ears, the shine of her lipstick and the flowing dress she wore suddenly made the kitchen seem old and decrepit.

"No problem. Come in," Cody said, pushing back the wooden chair he was sitting on a little too quickly. He caught it before it tipped and chose to ignore the little smirk his sister sent his way.

"I don't need to talk long," Vivienne assured him, flashing him a quick smile and smoothing her hair, pulled it away from her face. "I came to go over the menu for the next week with you. To make sure I'm on the right track."

"Of course. Yeah." He blinked, glancing around the kitchen, wishing he'd pushed Bonnie to clean up. Tonight he and Bonnie had taken their dinner and eaten it in the house. Something he tried to do from time to time.

"And I was wondering if I can have Bonnie help me tomorrow. I'd like to bake some snacks and desserts for next week."

Bonnie's face brightened and Cody bit his lip, thinking.

"You said I could help," Bonnie said, a whine entering her voice.

"Yeah. I know."

"I would have come and helped you tonight," Bonnie told Vivienne, "but Cody said I had too much homework. I'd love to help you tomorrow."

Vivienne's answering smile went right to his stomach, and right behind it came the memory of her sitting beside him in the truck on the way home. He'd had a hard time concentrating on his driving, what with her arm brushing his every time he turned a corner.

"And dinner was really good," Bonnie said with a surprising smile.

"Thanks. I'm glad you enjoyed it. I thought you might join us in the cookhouse, though."

Bonnie shrugged. "Cody doesn't like me eating with the hands too much. So sometimes I eat by myself. Sometimes we eat together."

Vivienne's nod and tight smile made Cody feel, once again, like an irresponsible brother. Balancing his need to be present for his sister and at the same time stay connected with his men was tricky. And frustrating, because he never felt like he was doing enough for either.

"Why are you going over the menu now?" he asked, unable to keep his annoyance from creeping into his voice. "You already bought the groceries."

He blamed his curt reply on the way she looked and the confusion she created. Sure, he was attracted to her. Who wouldn't be? Sure, she was beautiful.

But she was also the same kind of woman Tabitha was, and if Cody couldn't learn from the past, then he was dumber than some of his worst horses.

"I bought some basic staples. But I thought I could get anything extra I might need once we nail down the menu for the week."

Cody pulled a chair closer to the table, its legs screeching over the worn linoleum. "Okay. Let's see what you got," he said, wishing he hadn't been so pigheaded on insisting she do exactly what she was doing right now.

She gave him a tight nod, as if sensing his resistance to her, then with one easy and elegant motion, she smoothed her dress and sat down on the chair. Bonnie, ignoring her homework, leaned closer to look, as well. As Vivienne set the papers on the table, one of them caught on the bandage wrapped around her finger.

"How's the injury?" he asked, nodding at her bandage.

"It's fine. It's a nuisance to work with because of food safety, but I wrap it in plastic wrap." She stopped then laughed lightly. "Sorry. You don't need to know that." She turned her attention back to the menu. "One of the reasons I want to go over the menu with you is after dinner tonight, some of the men put in surprising requests of their own." She gave him a careful smile, which did nothing for his equilibrium. "I think there's a few gourmet chefs on your crew."

Cody ignored the little comment, looking down at the papers she held in her hands.

She laid a page on the table in front of him, her fingernail polish flashing in the light of the kitchen. "These are the breakfast menus for the next week. I tried to balance simple with tasty with some of the men's suggestions. And, of course, I will be making enough for everyone to have seconds."

Cody glanced at the papers with their neat writing and tidy columns and tried not to feel like an idiot. He didn't recognize some of the dishes she had written down, and what did it matter what she made as long as the men were satisfied?

But he had started this. May as well finish it. So he went through the motions of going over the breakfasts, suppers and which meals she would need Bonnie's help with.

He pointed to Sunday. "What's happening here?"

She frowned and leaned closer as if to get a better look. "Nothing different. Why?"

"We usually go to church Sunday. And even

though he wasn't always the best cook, Stimpy usually made a big Sunday dinner for all the hands after church."

"Of course. Sorry…I forgot." She looked sheepish. "Do all the men go to church?"

"Only the ones that want to. And we try not to work on Sunday. Give the men a day off."

"Really?"

"If it's too much work to do the dinner, you don't have to," Cody suggested.

"No. If that's what was done before, I'll do the same. Any suggestions?"

"I don't know." Cody glanced at Bonnie. "What did Mom always make?"

"Pot roast. When she was around. Which she isn't." Bonnie jumped to her feet and ran out of the room.

An uncomfortable silence followed this outburst. Vivienne kept her gaze on the papers in front of her, as if not sure what to say.

"Sorry about that," he said, apologizing for his sister's behavior. "She's been in a funk the past while. I'll have to go have a talk with her."

Vivienne ran her thumb along one edge of the papers, then glanced over at him. "I wouldn't be too hard on her," she said quietly. "I'm sure it's difficult for her to be away from your parents."

"I know. But it is what it is. She just has to make the best of it."

Vivienne looked like she wanted to say something more, but then she looked down at the papers in front of her.

"So I guess I can make pot roast on Sunday," Vivienne said quietly, making a note on the menu.

"Sounds good." Cody blew out his breath. "Look, thanks for coming and doing this, but I don't think you need to go over the menu with me next time."

"So you trust me to feed the men properly?" Vivienne said, a dimple teasing one cheek.

Cody frowned as he looked at her.

"What's wrong?" Vivienne asked.

He shook his head. "Nothing. For a moment… you reminded me of someone."

"Brooke?" she said with a light laugh.

"No. Someone else." He waved his hand as if dismissing the thought. "It's nothing."

Vivienne gave him a puzzled look, then gathered her papers together and stood. "So, I can count on Bonnie coming to help me tomorrow?"

"Yeah. That'd be okay. She doesn't have school, and any homework she has she can do at night."

"Okay. Thanks." Vivienne shuffled the papers together, then gave him a careful smile. "I…uh… have another favor to ask you."

"Sure. What do you need?"

"While I was at Brooke's place, Darlene Perry and her daughter, Macy, came by. Darlene said something about wanting Macy to learn how to cook, and one thing led to another, and, well…I was wondering if you would let me do a cooking class here. At the ranch."

"Why would you want to do that?" Cody asked, confused.

"I like cooking, obviously, and I thought it would be a nice thing to do for Darlene and Macy. I was thinking maybe next week, Saturday?"

"Why don't you do it in town?"

"I thought it would be more fun to do it here. There's more room, and being out on the ranch makes it like a retreat."

Cody wasn't sure what to think of this. The ranch wasn't a resort, but how could he say no without looking like a scrooge? Especially to someone like Darlene, who he knew had a pretty rough life.

He scratched his forehead, trying to puzzle this through.

"If it will cause too big a problem…"

He sighed then lifted his hands. "Okay. Sure. Go ahead."

Vivienne's broad smile brought out the dimple in her cheek and lit up her eyes. "Thanks so much. I really appreciate that."

Cody wished her smile didn't affect him. Wished it didn't make him feel kind of warm inside.

Because he knew Vivienne Clayton was a distraction he couldn't afford to indulge in.

Vivienne clutched the Bible as the minister spoke, feeling as if his words were directed to her and her alone. They gave her comfort and encouragement. For the first time in years she was sitting in church again, and it felt good to be here. Brooke, Gabe and A.J. were on one side of her in the pew, Zach and Kylie on the other.

Arabella and her boyfriend, Jonathan, sat two pews ahead of them with her triplet daughters and Jasmine and Cade, and directly in front of them sat Macy and Darlene.

She was surrounded by family, and for now, all was well in her world.

Reverend West spoke his final words, said "Amen," and as they rose for the final song, Vivienne's gaze stole across the aisle to where Cody stood beside his sister and his uncle Ted.

Cody held the songbook in one hand, his expression thoughtful as he turned the pages. When Cody had come to her cabin to pick her up for church, she'd had a hard time not staring. His hair, still damp from his shower, curled over his ears and neck. His blazer set off the breadth of his shoulders in a way his denim jackets and shirts didn't. He wore a white shirt under his blazer. No tie. Blue jeans and shiny cowboy boots.

She tore her attention away, reminding herself that he wasn't her type. The last man she dated wore a suit, tie and black loafers. Sophisticated. Elegant. Took her to plays on Broadway and dinners at Le Bernardin.

And bored you stiff and then dumped you.

She forced her attention back to the song, struggling to let the words enter her soul. It had been too long since she'd spent time with God. Too long since she'd let Him into her life.

She glanced over at Cody again, thinking of his parents. Missionaries. Good people. Christian people.

Her father had been emotionally distant and a workaholic. Her mother never got over their sister Lucy's death and suffered from depression.

Vivienne dismissed the thought as unkind. Her mother had her own difficulties. Being a widowed mother to three growing children had been a struggle and losing a child had to have been devastating.

Vivienne looked over at Cody again and, to her embarrassment, found him looking directly at her. They both looked away as Vivienne tried to suppress the flush warming her cheeks. What kind of person was she, eyeing up men in church?

The song was over and the minister pronounced the blessing and then they were done. Murmured conversation began and then swelled as people slowly moved out of the pews and down the aisle.

Brooke gave Vivienne a quick one-armed hug. "So, how did you like the service?"

"It was good," Vivienne said truthfully, returning her attention to the moment when she had felt a instant of connection to her past and her previous relationship with God. "I enjoyed it more than I thought I would."

Brooke gave Vivienne a bright smile. "It's so wonderful to be together as a family again. It seems like it's been decades since us Claytons worshipped together." Then a shadow crossed her face as if she were thinking of the ones who were missing.

Mei, who had suddenly stopped calling, not letting anyone know what her intentions were, was still living in San Francisco as far as anyone knew.

Zach had been keeping them up-to-date on what was going on with Lucas, but for the past week, he had nothing to report. It was as if Lucas had been swallowed up by the Florida Everglades.

Vivienne caught Brooke's hand in her own. "I'm sure Mei and Lucas will show up. We have to believe that."

Brooke nodded, but Vivienne saw the worry in

the lines around her mouth and the dull light in her eyes.

"I'll just have to keep praying," Brooke said quietly.

Vivienne was about to reply when Macy bounced up to join them, her grin as big as the oversize silk flower on her headband. "Hey there. You're going to teach me to cook, aren't you?"

"Yes, I am," Vivienne said, touching her finger to the little girl's nose.

Though she had only seen Macy once before, she felt a curious sense of protectiveness for the little girl. And who wouldn't? Vivienne knew what it was like to lose a mother, but she'd had a brother and sister to help her through. Macy had no one else in her life. Thankfully, Brooke and Zach had taken her under their wing and, when her mother passed on, they planned to adopt her. Brooke had told Vivienne how shy and withdrawn Macy used to be. Obviously being around the Claytons had helped the little girl come out of her shell.

"Mr. Jameson said we could use the cookhouse on the ranch this Saturday to do the lessons," she told the little girl.

Macy clapped her hands, her grin eclipsing the dimples in her cheeks. "I'm so excited."

Vivienne gave her a quick smile, then glanced over her shoulder.

"Looking for someone in particular?" Brooke leaned in close, her voice taking on a teasing note.

"Yes. My ride home," Vivienne said, angling her sister a warning look, hoping it covered her reaction. "I'm making Sunday dinner for the hands at the ranch, and I don't want to be late."

Brooke pouted. "I was hoping you could have dinner with us. Macy and Darlene are coming over and so are Zach and Kylie. We could have family time."

Yeah. Right. Family time with her very happy siblings and their significant others while she sat at the table obviously single. Pass.

"Sorry, sis. Can't be done," Vivienne said, gathering up her purse and coat, partially thankful she had a reasonable excuse. "But we'll see you all on Saturday at the ranch, okay?" She blew Arabella a kiss, waved at Zach, who was coming her way, then ducked out of the pew before anyone else in her family could waylay her.

But her passage out of the church was held up a few more times by people who remembered her and a few old classmates who had managed to stay around Clayton and find work.

She was about to slip out of the building when she heard her name being called.

She turned to see Reverend West walking toward her, waving his hand to catch her attention. Reverend West was a tall, bulky man in his forties with the build of a football player, but he easily caught up to her.

"Vivienne Clayton?" he asked, extending his hand, his brown eyes holding a welcome warmth. "I'm Reverend West, but you know that, of course. I thought I would introduce myself. Say hello."

"Nice to meet you," Vivienne said, shaking his hand. "Thanks for the sermon. I really appreciated what you said about forgiveness. Gave me a lot to think about."

Reverend West beamed. "Glad to know someone was listening. Sometimes I wonder." He shook his head, then pulled his attention back to her. "Anyhow, like I said, I just wanted to say hello. Welcome you back to Clayton. I also want to say I know what brings you back home."

A flush warmed her cheeks. It was money, pure and simple, and standing in front of this godly man made her feel somewhat tawdry.

"I know what your grandfather was like," he continued. "But I also know that he changed in the last few months of his life. And his will was a way of making amends to all his relatives by bringing a scattered and broken family back together." He released a light sigh. "I know he wasn't always the best person, but I need to tell you that he felt terrible for not helping your mother financially after your father died. For virtually ignoring her. He made his peace with God, and I hope you can learn to make your peace with your grandfather. Even though it might seem his last actions were manipulative, he did truly care about you all."

Reverend West's words kindled a curious warmth. "Thank you for that. I know he asked us to think kindly of him, to find one good memory. I know I have a few."

Reverend West nodded. "Then think on those. And if you ever want to talk, stop in at the church. I'm in my study most days, when I'm not visiting parishioners or doing something with the Church Care Committee." He brightened. "If you are at loose ends and have time to volunteer, we'd love to have you on board the Committee, as well."

"I'll see," was all Vivienne could say. "It might be difficult, given that I'm working full-time at the Circle C. But I'll keep it in mind." She gave him a quick smile, then turned and left the church, his words giving her much to think about.

Cody and Bonnie were waiting in the truck when she got there. Thankfully this time, Bonnie scooted over, giving her the seat by the window.

On the way up here, once again she had ended

up sitting beside Cody, and this time it was even more awkward than the first. She wished she could dismiss the feelings he evoked in her, so being able to sit by the window this time was a blessing.

Cody started up the truck, reversed out of the parking lot and headed down Eagle Street past the park.

"So what did you think of the service?" Cody asked as he made the last turn to the outskirts of town.

"I enjoyed it," Vivienne said quietly, clutching the handles of her purse. "Gave me lots to think about."

"We're lucky to have a minister as good as Reverend West in a town the size of Clayton."

"He seems like a godly man. And a very caring one," Vivienne replied.

Silence followed that observation and the only sound in the cab was the ticking of gravel against the truck's body and the faint strains of country music coming from the radio.

"I noticed a few of the hands in church." Vivienne spoke up after a while, trying to fill the awkward quiet.

"My uncle, of course. Grady and Delores always come. And Cade."

"He and his half brother, Jack, are the only

children or grandchildren of great uncle Samuel that bother showing up." Vivienne had a hard time keeping the harsh note out of her voice. Thinking kindly of her grandfather was difficult enough, but trying to find any good in the cousins on the Samuel Clayton side of the family was a real stretch. Especially after hearing some of the things Brooke, Zach and Arabella went through with their cousins in the past few months.

"He's good people," Cody said, his voice holding a stern note.

"I hope so. He's engaged to my cousin's ward, Jasmine. Arabella thinks the world of her," Vivienne said quietly.

"So what's the deal with you Claytons anyway?" Bonnie asked. "I thought you were all related, yet I sure don't think you all get along."

"We are related," Vivienne said, watching out the window as fields gave way to spruce trees. "But there's bad blood between the descendants of Samuel Clayton and his brother, George Clayton Senior, my grandfather."

"I heard that your grandfather wasn't such a good man. A friend of mine called him a shyster lawyer."

"Bonnie," Cody said, shooting his sister a frown. "You shouldn't speak ill of the man. He's not here to defend himself."

Vivienne had to smile at the old-fashioned courtesy Cody extended a man of her grandfather's questionable reputation.

"Grandpa George had his good points," Vivienne said quietly, thinking back to what Reverend West had said and the video shown after her grandfather's funeral. How Grandpa George had pleaded with each of his grandchildren to find one good memory of him. "I know he was the one who encouraged me to go to cooking school. Sometimes he would come over to my mother's place after my father died, and he always had something encouraging to say about my cooking."

Vivienne had to smile as she allowed the good memory to seep back into her mind.

"I guess that's good, then," Bonnie said. "I'm just glad that all us Jamesons get along."

The rest of the trip was made in silence, as if each of the people in the cab were caught up in their own thoughts. But though Vivienne was sitting on the other side of the truck from Cody, she couldn't help but wonder about his family. About his relationship with his parents.

Of how he frowned as he drove. And how he tapped the steering wheel whenever he had to wait.

She pushed her fickle thoughts back to what Reverend West preached about this morning. But even as she tried, her gaze kept slipping over to the man behind the wheel of the truck.

A while later when Cody parked his truck at the ranch, Vivienne couldn't get out of the truck fast enough.

"Thanks for the ride," Vivienne said before she left for the cookhouse. But before she could escape she had to ask another question. "Will you be joining the hands for dinner?"

"Can we?" Bonnie asked, grabbing her brother's arm. "I don't want to sit in the house by ourselves again."

Cody frowned, tapping his fingers on the steering wheel. "I suppose we could."

"Great." Bonnie shot a quick grin at Vivienne. "Then we'll see you later. I'm looking forward to pot roast."

Vivienne smiled at the girl's enthusiasm over the meal. "Okay," she said with a grin.

Bonnie hopped out of the truck and fairly danced toward the house.

But as Vivienne glanced at Cody, she caught him watching Bonnie with a glower. Then his gaze slid toward Vivienne and his frown deepened.

He got out of the truck and without a backward glance strode toward his house, as well.

Vivienne watched him leave, wondering what

was wrong with him. Which, in turn, made her wonder why she cared. He was just her boss. Nothing more.

She would do well to remember that.

Chapter Seven

"That's the third time she's been out for a walk this week." Grady angled his chin toward the slim figure in the bright yellow jacket making her way across the yard. "She went out Sunday, then Monday, now today."

Cody, standing outside the corrals, shot another glance Vivienne's way. She wore a skirt again today and a pair of tall boots with ridiculously high heels. Totally unsuitable for trekking around the ranch.

She probably would fit in on any street in New York. Here, she kind of stuck out.

"City girl," he said, projecting a note of disdain in his voice. It was the only way he could think of to stifle the lift that the "city girl's" appearance gave him. "I wish she'd stay away from the corrals, though. Every time she goes over, she spooks the horses with that bright coat of hers."

"Yeah. She certainly don't fit into ranch life," Grady said, pounding another nail into the corral fence he and Cody were fixing up. They were getting ready for the fall gather and the strength of the corral boards would get tested over the next couple of weeks. "Though she sure can cook. That French toast she made this morning..." Grady's voice trailed off as if remembering. "Maybe Delores can get the recipe."

"Why couldn't she just make porridge?" Cody grumbled.

Grady nudged Cody with his elbow. "Yeah, right. Like you'd eat porridge."

"Eaten enough of it. It's just food." Cody shrugged, glancing Vivienne's way again. This time, instead of heading toward the road, she was coming their way.

He tried not to watch, but as she came closer she tugged her ponytail loose. She pulled off her hat, then tucked it in her pocket. She ran her hands through her hair, letting it flow over her shoulder. Then, to Cody's disappointment, she pulled it back again and tied it up.

"Hey, boss. What should we do now?"

Bryce and Cade popped into his vision, cutting off his view of Vivienne.

"Um. Yeah." He straightened and dropped his hammer into the metal hanger on his carpenter belt, yanking his attention back to the work at hand. "You two can go help Ted in the machine shed. He's fixing the Massey. The clutch has been slipping. And bring him the John Deere, too. He said he wanted to look it over, as well." Cody shifted his hat on his head and tried to ignore Grady's smirk. His hired hand obviously caught him staring at Vivienne.

"So when do we head up to the hills?" Bryce was asking.

"I want to work with the horses and make sure the tractors are ready. We have to move some feeders and haul more hay before we get them." Cody planned as he spoke, thinking of the work ahead of him. "So in a couple of days. End of the week for sure."

Bryce nodded, then glanced back as Vivienne came closer. He grinned as he tipped his hat. "Afternoon, Ms. Vivienne," he said. "Surprised to see you out and about."

Cody caught sarcasm in the boy's voice that didn't sit right with him. Then he looked over to Vivienne now standing on the other side of the corral fence, her ponytail resting on one shoulder, her blue eyes shining, and he figured maybe the boy was just uncomfortable around her.

And why wouldn't Bryce be? Cody sure was.

"I go out every day," she said, her smile deepening the dimple in her cheek. Reminding him too much of the girl he'd been so stupid crazy about all those years ago.

He yanked a handful of nails out of his pouch, dropping a couple in the process.

As he bent over, he cursed his own clumsiness. This was ridiculous. He was a widower. He had tasted life with a girl like Vivienne, and look at the world of hurt that caused.

Stay on target, he reminded himself. *You've got responsibilities that you can't afford to get distracted from. She'll be here a year, and then she's gone.*

He straightened and ended up looking directly at Vivienne.

"What can I do for you?" he asked brusquely.

Her smile faded, and for a moment he regretted his defensive tone.

"I was just out for a walk and was wondering what you were doing."

"Just fixin' the corral." He fitted a nail into a board and started pounding it in, hoping he didn't hit his finger at the same time. "Some of the boards are loose, and before we get all the cows in here, I want to make sure they can't get out. Just have a real rodeo on our hands then."

And stop the babbling, or she'll think you're a bigger idiot than you are.

"Miss Vivienne, I heard that you're giving

cooking classes on Saturday," Cade said as Cody drove the nail home.

"Yes, I am. My sister, Darlene and Macy are coming up," she said in that singsongy voice of hers.

"My girl Jasmine heard about the classes from Arabella, who heard from Brooke. You know the Clayton telegraph," he said with an apologetic note. "But she was hoping she could come, too."

Grady straightened. "Cooking classes? You're teaching cooking classes? Can my wife come?"

"I suppose…" Vivienne's voice trailed off, and as Cody worked he caught her glancing at him. "If it's okay with Cody."

He shrugged, then glanced away. "Fine by me." It wasn't really fine. He wasn't too crazy about having a bunch of women taking over the ranch. Traipsing around and causing problems.

"What about us men?" Grady asked. "What if we want to take cooking?"

"Maybe another time," Vivienne said. "After all, according to Bonnie, there's not lots going on during the wintertime. I could do a few gourmet cooking classes for the guys."

"If it's boredom that's a problem, I'm sure Ted and I can come up with a bunch of things to keep you boys busy," Cody said, glaring as he straightened again. This girl and her city ways were obviously more of an inconvenience than he'd thought.

Bryce heaved a sigh, then headed over to the machine shed where Ted was working. Cade, however, lingered a moment.

"So, it's okay Jasmine comes?" he asked, his hands strung up in the back pockets of his blue jeans, his eyes intent on Vivienne.

"Of course Jasmine can come," Vivienne said kindly.

"Great. I'll tell her," Cade said. "Thanks, Miss Vivienne."

Vivienne turned to Cody after Cade took off. "I…uh…have another little favor to ask you."

So that was the real reason she came walking this way.

Did you think it was because she was drawn to your rugged appeal?

"Shoot," he said, digging in his carpenter's pouch for more nails and stabbing his thumb in the process.

"Bonnie wanted to take the cooking classes, too. I wanted to make sure it was okay with you."

"Yeah. Sure. Whatever."

"Great. She was asking, and I'm sure she'll be pleased." Her bright smile melted some of the defenses he'd put around his heart.

"Having a happy Bonnie around does make my life easier," Cody admitted. He heaved a board in place, trying to hide the discomfort he felt around her, then started nailing again.

"Okay, then." She hovered for a moment, as if she wanted to say something more, but then turned and walked away. Cody didn't realize he was watching her leave until Grady jabbed him in the ribs with the butt end of his hammer. "Time's a wastin', boss," he said with a broad wink. "You can see her tonight at dinner."

Except he was eating with Bonnie in the house again, so he wouldn't see Vivienne then.

He heard the sound of the John Deere starting up. At least Bryce was doing what Cody had asked him to.

He turned his attention back to his work. He had best focus on the ranch and not on Vivienne.

Right.

He pounded some more nails into the board, then he and Grady moved along, checking the rest of the corral system. They found a few more rotten boards, and as he and Grady were pulling them loose he heard the sound of yelling. And right behind that the rumble of hoofbeats and the whinny of horses.

What in the world? He straightened, glancing around.

"Horses are out. Horses are out," he heard Vivienne yell. "Somebody stop them."

What was going on? What was Vivienne saying?

Cody whipped off his carpenter apron and

vaulted over the corral in time to see half his horse herd come thundering past, heads and tails up as if reveling in their newfound freedom.

No time for this, he thought, watching them head past the cookhouse and around the bend in the road, dust swirling in their wake.

He spun around in time to see Bryce yank off his hat and throw it on the ground. Then he saw Vivienne standing by the fence of the pasture, the metal gate leading into it swinging back and forth, wide open.

"How did they get out?" Cody called out, jogging toward them. "What's going on?"

Vivienne opened her mouth as if to say something, then glanced over at Bryce, who was still shaking his head.

"She let the horses out," Bryce was saying.

"The gate wasn't latched properly," Cade put in.

"I told you to shut it after you," Bryce said, glaring at Cade.

"I did," Cade retorted.

Vivienne looked from Bryce to Cade to Cody, her eyes wide as if still unsure of what had happened.

"I was just talking to the horses in the pasture, like I always do," she said, turning to Cody. "But one of the horses was on its side. It looked like it was dead. So I told Bryce and Bryce told me to go see if it was breathing, then go get him. So I climbed over the fence, and went in to see if it was okay," she said. "And then I heard a loud noise and they got jumpy and ran around. And then one of them hit the gate and it opened and they all ran out. And then I yelled."

Her face was white, and Cody guessed she got a good scare.

But still…

He bit back his anger. It wasn't really her fault.

But still…

What was she thinking going into the corral, and what was Bryce thinking telling her to go check on the horse?

"Okay, Bryce, saddle up three horses," he barked. "You, Cade and Dover go round up the runaways."

"But I thought I was supposed to help Ted," Bryce complained.

"Just get those horses before they head into town," Cody snapped. He spun around, frustrated with both of them, and came face-to-face with Vivienne. She had her hands folded over that silly yellow coat of hers and she was biting her lip.

"Is there anything I can do?" she asked.

He scratched his temple with his forefinger, his anger fading away at the concern on her face.

"It was my fault they got out," she continued in a wavery voice. "I should do something to help."

He released a short laugh. "Don't worry about it. It was an accident. You didn't know what would happen."

She twisted her hands, glancing past him to the open gate. "I feel really stupid. I shouldn't have gone into the corral to look at that horse, but I thought I could help." She turned back to him, her expression pleading, as if hoping he believed her.

He wanted to pat her on the shoulder. Actually, he wanted to do more than pat her on the shoulder, but he kept his reaction down to a wry smile. "Don't worry. Just make sure you stay out of the way when they come back with the horses. They can be unpredictable when they're worked up."

"Okay. And I'm sorry. Again." She lowered her head and walked away looking so forlorn, Cody had to resist the urge to run after her and give her a hug.

"So then we pour the water-and-raisin mixture overtop and bake it." Vivienne opened the oven door and Macy carefully placed the pan holding the raisin pudding in the oven.

The kitchen was full of chattering, happy women, and Vivienne was pleased with how the cooking class was coming along. Pleased that Darlene could come and pleased Bonnie was in such good spirits.

"That's really easy," Macy said, looking proud of herself as Vivienne closed the oven door. Her mother, sitting on a chair by the butcher-block cutting board, was smiling, as well.

Vivienne gave Macy a timer and instructed her to set it for thirty minutes, then glanced out the window above the sink. From here she could see the horse pasture. From what she could tell, the horses were all still inside.

She still wasn't sure what had happened the other day, only that she should never have gone into the corral as Bryce had told her to. She was a city girl. What did she know about horses? It was just that she wanted to feel as if she could help, that was all. But it was almost as if Bryce had been playing some kind of game with her when he told her to check on the horse. At the same time, could Cade have been the one to leave gate open, as Bryce had said?

Her mind was a whirl of confusion. As she got to know Cade better this kind of thing seemed too out of character for the earnest young man who had won Jasmine's heart.

Still, was it possible that someone at the ranch had opened the gate? Had someone made that loud noise that had scared the horses?

She turned to Bonnie. "When you're finished with those peppers, I want you to sauté them with the sweet potato and the onions for about five minutes."

Jasmine sniffed as she sliced the onions. "There's got to be a way to cut these without my eyes watering so much."

"You could wear goggles," Vivienne said with a grin. As she rolled up her sleeves she glanced over to the stove, where Brooke worked. "Just cut that sweet potato up into one-inch cubes and give it to Brooke," she called out while she washed her hands and then punched dough she had rising for buns.

"My goodness, how do you keep all this straight?" Darlene asked, shaking her head as she glanced around the busy kitchen.

"In my job back in New York, I was used to being in control of a lot of chaos and a lot of egos." Vivienne laughed as she kneaded the dough.

Darlene sighed, wrapping her sweater more tightly around herself. "I would love to see New York sometime. Broadway, Central Park, Times Square."

"Bloomingdale's, Barneys, Saks," Vivienne added with a nostalgic sigh as she formed the buns.

"What do you miss the most about New York?" Jasmine asked as she sniffed again.

Vivienne paused, thinking. "Actually, I haven't

thought about New York for a while. I guess my work on the ranch has occupied most of my thoughts."

"How could this dump make you forget about New York?" Bonnie said, making a face.

"This isn't a dump," Vivienne corrected. "Your brother and uncle have built up a lovely place. Your house is beautiful. And the mountains surrounding the ranch make it seem like they are watching over it." Bonnie didn't look convinced, but Vivienne got an odd look from Brooke.

Vivienne ignored her smirk, directing the rest of the soup-making operation. "Jasmine, you can put your onions in the pan with the sweet potato and add some of those jalapenos you chopped."

"By the way, thanks for letting me come," Jasmine said. "Cade said he felt silly asking, but I'm glad he did. He's such a great guy."

A tinge of doubt niggled into Vivienne's mind. But she pushed it away. Cade was a good person.

"So, Jasmine, how are the wedding plans coming?" Darlene asked, cuddling Macy, who was perched on her lap eating a cookie.

Jasmine bit her lip, looking down at her hand and the ring encircling her third finger. "They're coming along, though Cade's brother Jack seems to want us to wait awhile."

"Why?" Brooke asked.

Jasmine's only answer was a gentle shrug. "Jack

is concerned about their stepfather, Charley. He thinks that he could cause problems."

"Why would he think that?" Brooke's voice held a sharp note that made Vivienne look over at her. Was something else going on that she didn't know about?

"I'm not sure. I know things aren't great between Jack and Cade and their stepfather, but I can't see why Jack thinks we should put off our wedding because of that." Jasmine's voice trembled a moment and Vivienne felt sorry for her. Though she'd had her own initial reservations about Cade, she'd since come to realize what a great guy he was. Now it didn't seem fair for these two innocent young people to be caught between the two families and their differences.

She went to Jasmine's side and slipped a comforting arm around her slender shoulders. "You and Cade love each other and you have to make your own decisions, apart from family," she said quietly.

Jasmine looked up then, her eyes shining with gratitude. "Thanks for that."

"Anytime."

Jasmine slipped her brown hair back over her shoulder. "Actually, I had another reason to come to this cooking class," she said shyly, looking up at Vivienne. "I was hoping to ask you to cater the wedding."

Vivienne glanced from Jasmine to Brooke as a tiny flutter of panic began. Cater a wedding? In her old hometown? What if she made the same mistake she had at the wedding that had cost her her job? What if she made herself look foolish in front of all the people she had grown up with?

She wiped suddenly trembling hands over her apron, pushing aside the self-defeating questions. "I…I'm not sure."

"That's okay. You don't have to," Jasmine hastily assured her. "It was just a silly idea. I've been hearing from Cade what a fantastic cook you are and how he's afraid he'll gain weight while working here, but I understand if you can't."

"Me and Arabella could help you, Vivienne," Brooke put in, her frown showing Vivienne what she thought of her sister's refusal. "You wouldn't have to do all the work yourself."

Vivienne still wasn't sure. "I don't know if I can."

"Of course you can," Brooke said. "You're an amazing cook. Always were."

Her sister's defense of her warmed her heart, and Vivienne knew she was coming across as uncooperative. Brooke couldn't know how badly being fired from her previous job had shaken her confidence.

"It would be great if you could help out," Brooke continued. "It wouldn't have to be fancy, but I know you could do a great job even if it's just hot dogs and buns."

Vivienne still wavered, but when she looked at Jasmine's disappointed face she made a reluctant decision. "Okay. I think I can do it," Vivienne said, forcing a smile, hoping she looked enthusiastic about the idea. "But I'll need help."

"I told you. You've got it," Brooke put in.

Jasmine's broad smile showed relief as well as happiness, and Vivienne felt a flush of pleasure. It would be okay, she told herself. It was no different than feeding the cowboys.

Except more public and with more stress.

"You should get Vivienne to do your makeup, too," Bonnie suggested, washing her hands in the sink.

"I think Vivienne will have enough to do with the cooking," Brooke intervened. "But maybe she could give you some pointers," Brooke said to Jasmine.

Bonnie looked up, then clapped her hands, her eyes bright. "I have an idea. Why don't we do makeovers?"

"That sounds like fun," Darlene said with a smile.

Vivienne glanced at Darlene with her pale skin and sunken eyes. If anyone could benefit from a makeover, it would be the poor woman.

Vivienne wiped her hands on her apron and

glanced at the clock. "We have time before the soup is ready. Why not?"

And fifteen minutes later, pots of eye shadow, tubes of mascara, bottles of foundation, cakes of blush and brushes of all sort lay strewn out on the table of the cookhouse along with Vivienne's curling irons, straighteners and brushes.

Giggles and bubbling laughter floated through the cookhouse as they experimented. When Vivienne saw Bonnie getting too heavy-handed with the colors, she took the brush away from her and showed her what she should do.

As Vivienne demonstrated, Bonnie inspected Vivienne's work in the hand mirror.

"Okay. I get it," she said, touching her forefinger to the corner of her eyes. "Cody always tells me I wear too much makeup. He says that when I'm older, I should try to wear makeup like you do." She gave Vivienne a coy smile. "He said you always look pretty. Without trying too hard."

Vivienne was dismayed to feel a flush warm her cheeks. Why should she care what Cody said to his little sister about her? Why should she care that he was paying her compliments?

But she did.

"I'm glad." Vivienne picked up a pencil and slipped the top off, pulling herself back to her task. "Now just a bit of eyeliner in a darker color, mascara, and there's the eyes."

Brooke looked up from what she was doing with Macy as Vivienne applied the blush. "Wow, Bonnie. That looks really good."

"It does, doesn't it." Bonnie's eyes shone up at Vivienne. "So what can I do about my hair?"

Vivienne turned on the curling iron, and they all moved onto the next phase of the makeover.

An hour later, five elegantly made-up woman sat around the table of the cookhouse, looking quite pleased with themselves.

"I believe this is the nicest I've looked in years," Darlene said with a giggle, patting the curls Brooke had put in her hair. She held up the mirror, smiling at her reflection.

"Do I look pretty?" Macy asked, slipping her glasses back on her face after Vivienne tied up her hair in a ribbon.

Vivienne leaned closer so she could look at her and Macy's reflection at once. "You look as beautiful as a princess," she said.

"Wow, look at you two," Bonnie said. "You look like you could be related with your blond hair and blue eyes."

Macy looked up at Vivienne, her eyes a shining lantern of trust. "I wish you could be my sister."

Vivienne smiled and tweaked the little girl's hair ribbon. "You know what? We can be sisters of the heart."

Macy's grin almost reached her ears. "I like that. Sisters of the heart."

Darlene dropped the mirror she was holding and Vivienne bent over to pick it up. "Are you okay?" she asked, noting the sudden paleness of the woman's cheeks.

"I'm fine," she replied breathlessly. "I'm just tired."

"We should think about leaving," Brooke said, closing up the compact she'd been using.

Vivienne got up and swept her own curled hair back into a ponytail. "I'll package everything up."

"This was really great," Jasmine said, cleaning up the pots of makeup. "Thanks so much. I really appreciate you catering the wedding. I hope…I hope it's not too much trouble. It won't be a large wedding."

Vivienne waved off her objections with a confidence she was still trying to muster. "It will work out fine." Though she had her reservations as to how a wedding between two vastly different sides of the Clayton family would turn out, now was not the time to state her concerns.

"Cade is working in the barn with Uncle Ted," Bonnie said, catching Jasmine's arm and giving it a tug. "Why don't you go show him how you look?"

Jasmine glanced at Brooke, who waved her off.

"Go. Give Cade a preview of how gorgeous you'll be at the wedding."

Jasmine slipped on a jacket, fluffed her hair and fairly flew out of the cookhouse. Bonnie was right behind her, bubbling with excitement.

Vivienne wondered at Bonnie's sudden enthusiasm but put it down to the busyness and excitement of having other people around.

"So, let's get the food packed up and you all can be on your way." As Vivienne walked to the kitchen, Brooke pulled her aside and gave her a quick hug. "Thanks so much for doing this class," she said. "I don't know if you realize how much it meant to Darlene and to Jasmine. And don't worry about the wedding dinner. Like I said, we can all help you." Brooke's smile was encouraging and gave Vivienne a sense of family and community that she had missed while she was so far away.

"I'll call you out on that. I'll need all the help I can get. But for now, come and help me get the food packed up."

As they worked, what Jasmine had said about their cousin Jack niggled at Vivienne.

"What's the matter?" Brooke asked as she placed a container in one of the boxes that Vivienne had scrounged up.

Vivienne frowned as she concentrated on snapping a lid on one of the soup containers. "I'm thinking about Jasmine's concerns about Jack wanting to convince Cade to stop the wedding. What's your take on Jack?"

Brooke sighed and shook her head. "Jack is a bit of a wild card. He just moved back to Clayton. I heard he is working as a wildlife biologist, so it's not like he's anything like his worthless father. In fact, just a couple of days ago I saw Charley tie into Cade and Jack stepped in to stop him. Yet, at the same time, Zach has said that he's seen Jack hanging around with Vincent."

"Well, they are cousins," Vivienne pointed out, wiping a drip of soup from one of the containers before she put it in the box Brooke was packing up.

"Sort of. Charley is Jack's stepfather, so that would make them stepcousins, I guess. But Charley won't win any father-of-the-year prizes, that's for sure." Brooke folded the flaps of the cardboard box over themselves, sealing it shut. "And I know Charley is no fan of our side of the family, either."

Vivienne sighed. "Grandpa George sure started something when he set this will up, didn't he?"

Brooke shrugged. "Probably, but I think we have to make sure we don't get pulled into it. And we have to make sure we keeping praying for our other cousins. God can do amazing things," she said.

* * *

Half an hour later, the kitchen was cleaned up and the makeup put back in her large cosmetic bag. Brooke, Macy and Darlene then left the cookhouse to get Jasmine and head home. Vivienne was getting food ready for dinner, a song in her heart as she glanced out the kitchen window, watching Jasmine going to Brooke's car.

A prayer bubbled up from her lips as Jasmine tossed a wave her way, got into the car and they all left.

Thank you, Lord. Thank you for family and community. And for a chance to help someone else.

She turned back to the kitchen and picked up the pail of potatoes to peel for supper when the door of the kitchen burst open.

Cody strode inside, his chaps flapping against his legs, his hat sitting skewed on his head. He stopped in the middle of the room, his hands planted on his hips and his eyes snapping.

"What did you do to my sister?" he demanded.

Chapter Eight

As his angry words echoed in the silence of the cookhouse, Cody realized how dramatic he sounded. But he was angry.

And, if he was fully honest with himself, a bit scared.

Just a few moments ago, two stunning young women strolled across the yard, and it wasn't until they got to the corral where he and Grady were working that he recognized Jasmine Turner.

And his little sister.

Instead of her overly done makeup, which usually made her look comical, Bonnie's eyes looked smoky and mysterious, her cheeks held a faint blush and her glistening lips had a pouty, glamorous look. Her hair hung to one side, pulled back from her face with a flower clip finishing the look.

She looked more like a fashion model than his little sister.

From the expression on Bryce's face, Cody could tell he thought the same. Which made him scared and angry at the same time.

"I don't understand. What are you talking about?" Vivienne looked genuinely puzzled, which kind of annoyed Cody. As if she didn't know what she had just done to his sister. The transformation she had effected.

"Bonnie looks twenty-five instead of fourteen." He unclenched his fists and spread out his fingers in an attempt to relax. "You're turning her into some kind of glamour girl."

"It was just good fun," she said, adding a smile as if hoping he would play along.

"Fun? Tell that to my hired hand whose jaw I had to pick up from the dirt when he saw her."

Vivienne leaned back against the counter, crossing her arms over her chest. "I see."

Cody didn't know if he liked the way she said that. As if she knew something he didn't.

"Let me tell you what *I* saw," he continued, "I saw a glamorous city girl."

"Like me?" A faint smile played around Vivienne's mouth, but her voice sounded hurt.

This *was* going all wrong. He shifted his weight on his hip, chewing on his lip, digging for the words to explain what he felt.

"My parents are ordinary people who are trying to serve the Lord, and I know they wouldn't approve." That wasn't what he was trying to say either, but he had to make Vivienne understand where he was coming from. She nodded for him to continue when he released a long, frustrated breath. "I don't want Bonnie getting any fancy ideas. We're plain folks, and that's all I want for her. I don't want her thinking that life is about looks. Life on the ranch is hard, and it's no place for…for someone who looks like my sister just did. She's too caught up in how she looks, and I don't want her getting ideas that will make it harder for her to live here." He stopped, trying to gather his thoughts. "And I don't like my hired hands making eyes at my little sister."

Vivienne tilted her head to one side, and the way she looked at him made him feel as if she were examining him like a specimen under a microscope.

"Does this have anything to do with your wife?" she asked, her voice quiet. "With Tabitha?"

He sliced the air with his hand. "Tabitha is gone. Has nothing to do with her."

"But she was a glamorous 'city' girl," Vivienne made little quote marks with her fingers when she said *city,* as if putting an extra emphasis on it. "And I'm wondering if you're worried that Bonnie will become that kind of person."

As her words permeated his frustrated anger, Cody could only stare at her. Then he blew out a sigh of resignation, but he wasn't ready to admit anything to Vivienne. Not yet.

Vivienne crossed her arms over her stomach, rocking back and forth as if thinking.

"Bonnie is just a young girl who was having fun with a bunch of other young girls," she said finally. "Girls do that when we get together. We do hair and nails and give each other fashion advice and we talk about the things that bother us. And maybe we put too much makeup on. And maybe it looks shallow and unimportant, but it's also a celebration of beauty. And life."

Cody fidgeted as her words slipped past his anger.

She pushed away from the sink, moving closer to him. "I like to think God gave us beauty to enjoy and appreciate. And that comes in different forms."

What she said made some kind of sense, but he didn't like the direction her conversation was taking. "I think the beauty God gave us should be natural," he said with a frown, trying to counter the argument. "Like what I see when I go outside. The trees, a summer storm. The way clouds race across the sky. The sight of a baby calf getting up for the first time on wobbly legs. I think that's the beauty God gives us to enjoy." He stopped himself there, suddenly self-conscious about what he was spouting off. He sounded like he should be writing a poem.

And when Vivienne smiled at him, he felt even sillier.

"That's beautiful," she said quietly, leaning her elbows on the counter between them. "I can see that you really love the ranch and ranch life."

"Always have," he said, his voice gruff. "That's who I am. That's who I'll always be."

He wished he didn't sound so defensive, but he felt as if he had to let Vivienne know—he was what he was.

"There's nothing superficial about you, is there?"

"What you see is what you get," he said.

Vivienne looked down at the counter, then traced a circle in the wood with her finger. "I like that about you," she said softly.

Cody couldn't formulate a reply. Her words confused him.

Then she lifted her head and looked directly at him. "I think Bonnie is lucky to have a brother like you," she murmured. "You're a good person, Cody Jameson."

Her simple words penetrated his soul and clouded his mind. He couldn't think of anything to say. So he just stood there, looking at her.

And she looked back, their gazes meshing.

Cody felt as if time slipped back and he was

once again that silly cowboy, hoping to get a date with the beautiful Vivienne Clayton.

Yet, as she held his gaze, something else was happening. Something hesitant and familiar. Something that made his heart speed up. Just a bit.

She looked like she was about to say something, when he pulled himself back to the now and reality. He slapped his hat on his head, spun around and strode out of the cookhouse as if outrunning what had just happened.

"Do you need me to do anything more?" Bonnie tossed the towel she had been using to dry the pots into the wash basket Vivienne had set in one corner of the kitchen.

Vivienne glanced around the tidy kitchen with a feeling of satisfaction. "No. I think we're done here."

Her Monday morning breakfast had been another success. She'd made scrambled eggs this time but had added bits of bacon, some onions, a few sautéed mushrooms. With them she'd served sausage biscuits and the usual gallons of coffee.

It was all gone, but enough was left over to show her she'd made the correct amount. When she served the food, however, she'd been disappointed to find out that Cody and Bonnie weren't there. Yesterday, at church, she'd hoped to talk to Cody, but only Bonnie and Uncle Ted had attended. Cody, apparently, had stayed back to get some work done.

He didn't come for lunch afterward, nor did he show up at suppertime.

If Vivienne was honest with herself, she knew Cody's absence bothered her because of that moment they shared on Saturday in the cookhouse. In spite of his anger with her over Bonnie's transformation, as they talked and as his anger passed, something else had slipped into the atmosphere.

And, to her surprise, she found she wanted to pursue the hesitant possibilities of that moment.

Bonnie smoothed down her hair and pressed her lips together, as if evening out the lipstick Vivienne had seen her put on before she started. Though Bonnie and Cody had eaten in their own house, as soon as they were done Bonnie had come to the cookhouse.

However, she didn't come directly to the kitchen, and when Vivienne had heard her voice and left the kitchen to investigate, she'd seen Bonnie chatting with Bryce.

Since then, Vivienne had been trying to find a way to bring up the subject of Bryce without making it look like she was prying, but she hadn't had much of a chance.

Bonnie had been full of prattle about school

and friends and all the things she would do once she got away from Clayton. How she would move to New York, like Vivienne had. How she would become a famous model and an actress on Broadway.

And on and on.

"So if you don't need me, I need to get ready for school," Bonnie said, moving toward the dining room door, as she fluffed her hair with her hands. "And I, uh, should say hi to Uncle Ted."

Vivienne knew exactly what Cody's little sister was up to. "Can I talk to you a minute before you go?" she asked, feeling guilty for what she started when she did the makeover on Saturday. Yesterday, at church, Bonnie had worn a floaty ivory dress over brown leggings. A silk flower was pinned in her hair, and her makeup was just the way Vivienne had taught her. Understated and elegant.

And too mature for her age.

Much as Vivienne hated to admit it, Cody was right. She hadn't done Bonnie any favors when she did the makeover with her.

Bonnie frowned as she tugged on her tank top and adjusted her sweater. Little fussy things a girl did before she saw someone she wanted to impress.

"Okay. But I don't want to miss the school bus."

"I thought you had to talk to Uncle Ted?" Vivienne asked, keeping her voice quiet, low-key.

"Well, yeah. I do." Bonnie fiddled with the one of the many necklaces she wore. "And then I have to catch the bus."

"And you won't make a little detour to see, let's say, Bryce?"

Her flaming cheeks told Vivienne everything she needed to know.

"Bonnie, you're only fourteen—"

"You sound just like Cody," Bonnie proclaimed, her glistening lips taking on a very adolescent pout. "He always says I'm too young."

"And Cody is right. You're too young to flirt with boys."

"I'm not flirting," Bonnie said, her pout growing.

Vivienne bit her own lip, wondering why she ever thought she could give this girl guidance. She walked around the counter, coming to stand between Bonnie and the doorway out of the kitchen. She took Bonnie's hands in hers and squeezed lightly, as if to let her know she cared.

"Cody cares a lot about you. He feels very responsible for you. If he tells you something, it's because he loves you, not because he's trying to make your life miserable."

Bonnie looked away, and Vivienne could see the young girl wasn't convinced. "If he loves me, why does he make me stay out here on the ranch even though I hate it?"

"Where would you sooner be?"

"Town. I hate living out in the country." Bonnie glanced at her. "You get it, don't you? You don't like it here either."

A few weeks ago Vivienne might have agreed...but now? She wasn't so sure. Not after spending time out here. Not after going for walks around the ranch. The peace and quiet and the beauty of the surroundings were settling into her soul.

"You used to live in New York," Bonnie continued. "That's where I want to be."

Vivienne latched on to that idea as a way to motivate Bonnie to hold back. "Okay, if you want to move to New York and if you want to make a life in the city, then you can't afford to get distracted by someone like Bryce." Someone who, Vivienne knew, Cody would definitely not approve of. Someone *she* didn't approve of. The boy's attitude, at times, bordered on insolent.

Bonnie caught her lower lip between her teeth, as if thinking.

"You need to keep your focus on what you really want," Vivienne urged. "Don't let guys be a distraction to your plans. Keep your eye on the prize."

Bonnie sighed and then glanced past Vivienne, and her frown deepened.

"I'm coming, Cody," Bonnie said, pulling her hands away from Vivienne.

Vivienne turned around and once again was the victim of Cody's scowl. Had he heard what she said to Bonnie? How must that have sounded in his ears?

But before she had a chance to say anything more, Cody ushered Bonnie out of the kitchen and left without a backward glance.

Vivienne watched them go, wondering why she felt a need to run after him to explain.

It doesn't matter, she told herself, spinning around and pulling out a cookbook she had found in the pantry.

She shouldn't care what he thought.

But as she flipped through the book, she knew she was fooling herself. The words she had told Bonnie, words she had simply used as a way of discouraging Bonnie's flirtation with Bryce, echoed in her head again and again. She knew how they must have sounded to Cody.

And why do you care?

When she heard the growl of a diesel engine, she looked up and saw the school bus heading down the driveway. Before she could change her mind she grabbed her coat, slipped it on and headed outside.

A light drizzle drifted against her face, moisture beading up on her eyelashes, making it difficult to see the mountains guarding the ranch.

She had gone out for a walk every day last week, just to get out of the cookhouse and to get some fresh air. Each time she did, the first thing her eyes sought and found was the rugged beauty of the mountains. Each day she went out she discovered something new and interesting and completely different from anything she'd ever see in the city.

One morning she saw a couple of deer grazing in the pasture, their large ears flicking in curiosity as they lifted their heads to look at her. When they had seen her, they simply turned and nonchalantly bounced away.

Another morning she had seen the sun shining through a cloud, the rays like silver beacons reaching to earth. She had stopped to look as the beams slowly dissipated and the sun appeared from behind the cloud.

Her mind had slipped back to something the pastor said about God revealing Himself in creation this past Sunday.

She knew what Cody meant by the beauty of nature, and she found that each day she spent on the ranch, she grew more aware of it. And it filled a part of her soul she didn't know was empty. Until she came to the Circle C.

As she made her way across the yard, she heard

Cody calling out to Bryce to bring him the next horse. She skirted a puddle, wishing she had taken a moment to put on her boots, but a sense of urgency had taken over her actions. Urgency she didn't want to examine and couldn't dismiss. She just knew she needed to talk to Cody as soon as possible.

She got to the corral just as Cody picked up one of the horse's feet and lifted it up, anchoring it between his knees. He wore his chaps, but his jacket hung from one of the corral posts. He had rolled up the sleeves of his shirt, and the soft drizzle had created rivulets of dirt running down his muscular forearms and into his leather gloves.

As he bent over, his hat hid his face.

Bryce handed Cody something and, curious, Vivienne came closer, standing on the first rung of the fence and hooking her elbows over the top rail so she could see better.

Though she wasn't raised on a ranch, she was enough of a small-town girl to recognize that Cody was shoeing the horse.

With quick, easy movements he got the shoe on, then Bryce handed him another tool and he cut off the ends of the nail protruding out the sides of the horse's hoof. Then with a rasp, he smoothed it all out.

He dropped the foot and arched his back, groaning. "Okay, let's do the next one," he said quietly, walking around the back of the horse, his hand sliding over the horse's rump. In a matter of minutes he had the back one done, as well.

As he straightened, he glanced over and their eyes met again.

But this time he looked away, walking to the front of the horse. He caught it by the halter rope and stroked its head, murmuring softly to it.

Then he led it away without a backward glance.

Disappointment lashed at her. Maybe she should just go. Cody would think of her what he wanted regardless of what she was about to tell him.

Then the Clayton stubbornness kicked in. She had come out to talk to Cody to set the record straight, and she would. That was all there was to it.

So she waited, watching as he unbuckled the halter, scratched the horse between the ears and with a light pat sent it on its way.

The other horses had gathered around and Cody rubbed this one, then that one, then took the halter he had just taken off the one horse and slowly approached a tall, brown horse. He held his hand up and then pressed his palm on the horse's head. Then he slid his hand around the horse's neck and slipped the rope around.

The horse tried to pull away, but Cody put his hand on the horse's nose again and the horse calmed down. "Easy, Amarillo. It's okay," he said, and the pitch and timbre of his voice made Vivienne feel as if everything was, indeed, okay.

A minute later, Cody had the halter on Amarillo and was leading him into the corral.

"Can't believe you got him," Bryce said. "He's always so skittish."

"Just got to make it easy for him to do what you want him to, hard for him to do what you don't want him to," was all Cody said. As he spoke he looked over at Vivienne, acknowledging her presence with a tight nod of his head.

Vivienne gave him a smile, but he was already looking away.

So she stayed and watched as Cody put shoes on this horse, as well. But by the fourth shoe, the horse grew restive and kept shifting and kicking away with his hoof.

One time Vivienne thought the horse would kick Cody, but he moved out of the way in time. But he could not get the horse to settle down.

"Open the gate to the round pen," he told Bryce, wiping a slick of sweat off his face with his forearm. He straightened, caught his breath and led the horse inside.

For the next few minutes, Cody made the horse run around and around him. Cody stood in the middle of the pen, flicking the horse occasionally with the end of a rope whenever he slowed the pace. The horse went around and around, then slowed down.

"You want to talk now?" Cody asked, flicking the rope at the horse again. "You ready to pay attention and listen?"

To Vivienne's amazement, the horse seemed to nod and Cody let it slow, then the horse came to him. Cody waited a moment, then clipped a rope to his halter and led the horse back.

Five minutes later Cody lowered the hoof, complete with shoe, and let Bryce lead him away to the pasture.

"Wow, that was interesting," Vivienne said aloud, trying to catch Cody's attention, ignoring her first desire to leave.

Cody glanced her way, took a breath and to her relief, walked over to her.

"So why did you make him run around the pen?" she asked, pressing her advantage now that she caught his attention.

"It's a way of showing him I'm the boss. Of showing him I'm in control of his situation." Cody rolled the sleeves of his shirt down and glanced back at the horse.

"How did you know when to stop making him run around?" Vivienne felt foolish, hanging around the corral, but she wanted to clear things up with Cody.

"When they start making those chewing motions with their mouth, it means they're ready to communicate. To submit."

Cody pushed his hat back on his head, his eyes on her.

Vivienne held his gaze, wishing she could find a way to say what she wanted to say and not sound foolish. One thing was certain: she wasn't about to make chewing motions with her mouth.

"About what you heard me say to Bonnie…" She paused. "I wasn't trying to make her dissatisfied with her life on the ranch. I wasn't trying to convince her that life in the city was better than life on the ranch." She stopped there, still not sure what she could say to erase the frown on Cody's face.

"So why did you tell her that? Encourage her to 'keep her eye on the prize,' in your words?" Cody's voice held a disturbing edge. As if something else she had said made him angry.

She caught her lower lip between her teeth, leaning forward so Bryce couldn't hear her.

"Over the past few of days, I've realized a couple of things, and I want to apologize. When I did the makeover with Bonnie, it was just good fun. But when I saw her flirting with Bryce and how Bryce seems attracted to her, I got nervous. And I didn't know how else to get her to stop or think about something else." Vivienne paused a moment, wishing that she dared to pray. Because right about now, as she looked into Cody's eyes, she felt she could use some divine intervention. "So I latched on to the one thing she's talked about over and over again. If she wants to move to the city, she shouldn't let Bryce be a distraction."

Cody held her gaze an extra beat, as if testing her sincerity.

"I was just using what she wanted to get her to do what I wanted. Kind of like you did with that horse. Made it easy for her to do what I wanted and hard for her to do what she thought she wanted. Kind of." She gave him a wry smile.

"So it wasn't about how much better city life is than country life?"

There it was again. That faint edge she couldn't identify. But she shook her head. "No…of course not. I keep telling her how lucky she is to live out here, though she thinks I'm kidding her."

Cody leaned his elbow on the rail of the fence, bringing him closer. "Is that the only reason you came out here? To tell me that?"

She shrugged, feeling a little bit silly, hanging on to the fence, Cody's arm inches from hers. But she didn't want to move away. Not yet.

"I'm heading out for a walk anyway, but thought I'd leave earlier." She chanced a quick sidelong glance, disconcerted to see him looking at her. "I wanted to catch you before you head out for the day. I just wanted to make sure there wasn't any misunderstanding. About what I said."

Cody's nod was accompanied by a slow grin. "I'm glad you came to talk to me. Glad we're on the same page where Bonnie is concerned." He pushed his hat back on his head with his gloved knuckle. "So you like going for a walk?"

She didn't want to look at him, but her gaze drifted to his and she was pleased to see him smiling at her.

"As long as I stay away from the horse pen."

"That wasn't your fault," he said, his voice low and quiet. "Just a mistake."

His assurance smoothed away her shame of that moment. "Thanks for that. And as for your other question, I really enjoy my walks around the ranch. Yesterday I saw a bald eagle. Haven't seen them for a while."

"I don't imagine they hang around the skyscrapers of Manhattan."

"Brooklyn, actually, but no. Not there either."

His light laugh encouraged her.

"It looked so majestic soaring above the mountains."

"What's really cool is riding up on some mountain trail and seeing an eagle or a hawk soaring above the trees, but below you. It makes a person feel pretty small."

She caught peace in his voice as he spoke. Contentment. He really was one with this place.

"That would be wonderful to see," she said quietly, suddenly jealous of his attachment to his roots.

She had grown up in Clayton, but for as long as she lived here, especially after her father died, all she could think of was leaving. Heading to a place where possibilities seemed endless. Where excitement seemed to linger around every corner.

She'd lived in Paris. She'd lived in New York.

But she never experienced the sense of home she heard in Cody's voice whenever he spoke of the ranch. As he told her the other day, what she saw is what she got.

And more and more she was liking what she saw.

She looked his way, their gazes locking, and once again hesitation trembled behind her realization. Then, to her consternation, Cody's gloved hand rested on hers. Leather lay between their hands, but the deliberate touch was oddly intimate.

"Maybe you'll have to come up into the hills sometime."

She tested the idea as a smile lingered on her lips. "I think I'd like that."

"Hey, Cody, what should I do with Amarillo?" Bryce called out, his voice breaking the moment.

Cody pulled away, and Vivienne stepped down from the rail. As she moved away from him, doubts and misgivings slipped back into her mind.

What was she doing? She had to follow her own advice. Keep her eye on the prize.

And how was she supposed to do that as long as she worked here? As long as she saw Cody every day?

Chapter Nine

Cody guided his horse down the trail, squinting in the dark. A trickle of water worked its way down his chilled neck and back. The drizzle that ended yesterday after he was done shoeing up the horses had turned into rain on his way down the mountain trail to the ranch.

He and the men had spent most of the day moving cows in the upper pasture in readiness to bring them down to the ranch. While they were riding through and gathering them up, he'd found a calf on its own. He'd told the men to go ahead, he'd go and find the mother. He didn't think it would take him long. He worked his way through some shin-tangle, then up into a gully where he finally found the cow. Somehow she'd gotten her front feet wound up in the scrub brush and couldn't get free.

By the time he got her cut loose and reunited

with the calf, it was dark and the men were long gone. And because he had left his slicker behind, he was soaked to the skin.

Yet, in spite of the general lousiness of the day and how damp he was, as he saw the lights of the ranch through the rain, anticipation stirred within him.

Vivienne was down there.

He tried to dismiss the thought, but since yesterday, when she'd come to the corral to talk to him about what he'd heard her say to Bonnie, he felt as if things had shifted between them.

It was as if his opinion of her mattered to her.

He had gone back and forth all day on that, trying to keep his mind on his work. Usually he didn't feel so scattered. Usually he could focus on the job at hand.

He tried to dismiss Vivienne simply as a distraction. The same thing she had warned Bonnie that Bryce was.

Trouble was, deep inside, he knew Vivienne was more than that. They say you never forget your first love. And Vivienne was the kind of person you didn't forget.

Even after she turned him down flat that day in high school, he couldn't put her completely out of his mind. She was always that elusive golden girl.

Once in a while, he even wondered if she was

the reason he was attracted to Tabitha. Because, on one level, she was a lot like Vivienne.

Tabitha had hurt him, too, he reminded himself as he guided his weary horse back to the corral. Tabitha had caused him pain and sorrow in so many ways. When she died, so much died with her.

He pushed the negative memories aside, recognizing them as unfair to a woman he had loved at one time. But they didn't disappear completely.

As he dismounted, water squished out of his drenched socks in his boots as he stepped onto the muddy ground of the corral.

He loosened the strap holding the cinch snug, the wet leather unyielding as the rain came down in a relentless sheet. His horse, Tango, stamped and snorted, splashing mud with his hooves, impatient to be free of the saddle and bridle.

By the time Cody had the strap loose, his hands were stiff and ice cold, his neck and back soaking wet.

"Hey, boss, you okay?" Cade called out from the darkness.

Cody looked up to see the young man clambering over the fence, illuminated by the light in the eave of the horse barn. What was he doing here?

"Yeah. I'm okay," Cody replied, pulling up the cinch and hooking it to the saddle horn. "Just got to get Tango's bridle and halter off and he can go out into the pasture."

"Let me do that," Cade said, taking the saddle from Cody. "You look frozen. Did you get that cow and calf mothered up again?"

Cody nodded, tugging off his wet gloves. "We'll have to wait until this rain lets up to move the cows. Trail's too muddy right now."

"I'm sure the guys don't mind a day of hanging around the ranch," Cade said with a grin as Cody took the halter off his horse.

"I doubt you'll be hanging out here," Cody said, walking through the mud and rain to the horse barn. "Imagine you'll be wanting to see Jasmine."

"Yes, I will," Cade said with a laugh as he hefted the saddle onto the saddle tree in the tack room. The odor of wet horse rose up and filled the small room.

"She's a great gal," Cody said, stringing up the halter beside the others, banging his head against the single lightbulb hanging from the ceiling. It sent their shadows dancing eerily along the wall. "Pretty, too."

"Inside and out," Cade replied, hanging the blanket on another rack. "Sometimes I don't feel like I deserve her."

Cody paused a moment, taking the young boy's measure. "You been getting any grief from Vivienne's family about marrying her?"

Cade shrugged, resting his hand on a saddle. "It's been kind of a Romeo and Juliet thing. Jasmine's family has been great."

"And your family?" Cody slapped his hat against his thigh then dropped it on his head, his growling stomach reminding him that he hadn't eaten since breakfast this morning.

"Vincent is being a jerk, but that's cousin Vincent," Cade said in a matter-of-fact tone. "Marsha and Billy Dean keep reminding me that the George Claytons are selfish and greedy, which is pretty rich coming from them." He gave Cody a quick grin, as if to ease away the sting of his comments. "Les is pretty apathetic about it all. My brother Jack doesn't say much. He's had his own troubles with both sides of the family, so he's kept his opinions to himself."

"Stick with it, Cade. You and Jasmine are lucky to have each other. It's not often you find someone you connect with." As soon as he spoke, Cody felt foolish. He sounded like the boy's uncle instead of his boss.

"You're right," Cade said with a shy smile. "We've both been blessed by each other, and I know people think we're a bit young to get married. I am thankful that the Lord brought us together."

"Any future plans?" Cody asked.

Cade gave a self-conscious shrug. "I'd like to go to medical school after Jasmine and I get married."

Cody clapped his hand on Cade's shoulder. "You're ambitious." And for a moment he was jealous of the young boy's conviction and his obvious love for his future wife.

Had he felt like that about Tabitha? He pushed the thoughts aside. Tabitha was gone, and it wasn't fair to go back and dissect that relationship.

"I better get out of these clothes," Cody said, heading out the door. "Try to scrounge something to eat at my house. I imagine everyone else is finished." His stomach growled again, wondering what treats Vivienne had cooked up that he had missed out on. Though he had told her over and over that he wanted her to serve simple food, she always found a way to make things extra tasty.

"Vivienne told us that if any of us saw you, she had supper waiting," Cade said as he closed the door.

"You ate already?"

Cade nodded.

"So what were you doing coming from the other side of the yard?"

"Thought I saw something and I was going to check it out when you came. Figured I better pass Vivienne's message on first. She's in the cookhouse now, cleaning up," Cade said, pulling up his collar against the rain as they walked across the yard. "Everyone else is gone, but she's still there, and I know she said she was keeping some food warm for you. Supper was really good, so it's worth taking time to get it."

Cody just nodded, thankful that the watery beam of the yard light was behind him, throwing his face into shadow. That way Cade couldn't see his anticipation.

The cookhouse was eerily quiet as Cody stepped inside. The tables were cleaned off and the floor swept. A single light glowed at one end, creating shadows. He paused a moment to take his wet coat off and hang it up. He glanced at the clean floor and toed his boots off. But as he walked across the floor to wash his hands, his wet socks left damp footprints on the wood. When he was done, he paused at the door to the kitchen, wishing he didn't feel this thrum of expectation. The sound of Vivienne's humming only increased it.

For a moment, he was tempted to turn around and leave. Spending time with Vivienne one-on-one maybe wasn't the best idea. But then his stomach rumbled and he heard Vivienne call out, "Anybody there?"

Busted.

So he squared his shoulders, told himself he

was just hungry, nothing more, and pushed through the swinging door into the kitchen.

Warmth and light greeted him, and he shivered. Then Vivienne was walking toward him, the overhead lights of the kitchen burnishing her hair into spun gold. Her smile was as bright as the sun, and the thrum became a steady beat.

"Cade told me…about dinner…" He cleared his throat and tried again. "Cade said you had dinner waiting for me."

Vivienne nodded. "I'm glad you came. You must be starving." She waggled her hand as if to motion him to follow her. "I've got your dinner in the oven, and I've set a place for you at the table in the corner."

Cody walked toward the table, set with a plate and cutlery, and when Vivienne opened the oven, the aroma of chicken almost made him faint.

"Here's your first course," she said, setting a large plate heaped with food in front of him.

Cody glanced down at the plate, the scent of chicken and stuffing and potatoes and beans filling his nostrils. Ordinary food, but the chicken looked like it had been breaded with something and the potatoes had been cubed, seasoned and baked. The beans glistened and were sprinkled with almonds, and the stuffing looked and smelled better than any stuffing his mother had made.

"Cade told me it was worth coming to the cookhouse for," he said, rubbing his hands over his damp jeans. "He was right."

Vivienne tossed him a quick smile over her shoulder as she walked to the refrigerator. She slid open the glass door and pulled out a jug of milk.

Cody inhaled the heady scent of his supper, then ducked his head and thanked God for the food. For the day. And asked God to make sure he didn't make a fool of himself in front of Vivienne.

Because her presence was more alluring than the most gourmet dinner she could have made.

She set a glass of milk in front of him and a glass of water.

Cody picked up the glass of water and toasted her with it. "To the cook, with grateful thanks."

"You just eat," she said, a flush staining her cheeks.

And for the next few moments, Cody allowed himself to enjoy to the fullest the meal Vivienne had served him. He had to catch himself from groaning with pleasure with each bite, it tasted so amazing.

"This is fantastic" was all he could mumble as he cut off another piece of chicken, trying to figure out what she had done to it. "I've never tasted anything like this before."

"Parmesan chicken. Secret recipe given to me by a fellow student in Paris," she said with a coy grin. She sat across the little table from him, which made him feel more awkward.

"You didn't have to do this," he said as he finished off the meal. Tabitha wasn't much of a cook, so even when he was married he had often eaten with the men, but his previous cook seldom, if ever, saved dinner for them. And if he did, it was usually a plate dished up and waiting on the counter, congealed, cold and unappealing.

He had never been waited on like this, and it didn't help that the person waiting on him was Vivienne Clayton.

She smiled at him, then took his plate when he was done. "You want some more?"

"It was delicious, but I'm full."

"Too full for dessert?"

He could only stare at her, open-mouthed. "Seriously?"

"Actually, it's apple pie, but I can give you a side of 'seriously' if that's what you prefer."

He laughed at that and lifted his hands. "What can I say? You've hit my soft spot."

"So I was told."

She came back with a generous wedge of apple pie, the crust flaky and light and a large scoop of ice cream on the side. The golden crust had flakes so fine you could see through them. And the aroma was, again, familiar and yet different.

"Gourmet apple pie," she said, setting the plate

in front of him with a flourish. "Enjoy." She poured him a cup of coffee, then poured one for herself and once again sat down across the table from him.

Before he took a bite of the pie, he looked across the table at her and felt a peculiar sense of home.

This feels right, he thought, hardly daring to examine the situation too closely. He was sitting across the table from Vivienne Clayton. She had just served him dinner and pie and was now sharing a cup of coffee with him. If someone would have told him—

"Did you find the cow?" she asked, cradling her mug between her hands, her head tipped slightly to one side.

"Yes, I did." He wiped his mouth and took a sip of scalding coffee that added an extra flush of warmth.

"I'm glad. The boys said you were worried."

"I don't like seeing orphaned calves," he said.

"I'm not surprised."

Cody wondered what she meant by that, but he didn't want to ask. He finished off the pie and resisted the urge to lick the plate.

"That was…amazing. Don't know how else to say it. Just a great dinner."

"And simple."

He cocked her a quick smile. "If you want to call it that."

"Hey, for me it was."

A comfortable silence followed her comment and as they drank their coffee Cody marveled that he could feel so at ease with her.

"So how was your day?" he asked, resting his elbows on the table, a move that brought him just a little closer to her.

"I cleaned out the freezer and discovered some interesting souvenirs from your previous cook."

He frowned.

"One of the men told me they are called prairie oysters in some circles."

Cody laughed. "Ah, yes. Stimpy kept threatening to serve us those. Never did."

"That you know of," she said with an impish grin.

He laughed again. She told him about a few other things she had discovered. He told her about the cow gather that was coming up. The conversation shifted from work to life. He asked her what the minister preached about on Sunday, and he was pleased to find out that she remembered.

The conversation grew easy and flowed from family to community to thoughts on God and hopes.

She got up and poured him another cup of coffee, and neither of them made any move to leave. As they talked Cody felt the attraction that had been just a whisper—just a thought—growing and shifting.

They were moving into new territory…and though he wasn't sure he knew his way around this place, he knew he didn't want to leave. Not yet.

When Vivienne came to sit down, her chair had moved a bit closer. Now they were practically side by side, their hands almost brushing each other whenever they put their coffee cups down.

She was laughing at something he said when a strand of hair got stuck on her lips.

Without thinking, he reached up and, slipping his fingers behind the hair, gently brushed it away. Then his hand was on her chin, his fingertips resting against her cheek.

She was looking up at him, her eyes wide, shining, her lips parted with…expectation?

He wasn't sure what, but he knew he couldn't simply sit here, his hand on her face, his eyes on hers.

He leaned closer, and she did, too.

Their lips met, warm and cool, soft and rough. His hand slipped to her neck, then down her back. Her hand came up and cupped his face, her other hand on his shoulder.

And then she was in his arms, she was holding him, and their kiss shifted and changed. She moved and laid her head on his chest, her one hand tangling in his damp hair.

A gentle sigh eased out of her and then she pressed her lips to his neck.

"Vivienne," he breathed, unable to say more than her name.

He wanted her closer, so he pulled her off her chair and onto his lap and she rested her head on his shoulder, her arms around him.

He closed his eyes with contentment. This was so right. He felt as if he had finally come home.

A sharp whistling pierced the intimate quiet, and Vivienne slowly drew away.

"It's the... I'm heating water... The kettle." She pushed her hair away from her face, then jumped off his lap and hurried to the stove, turning off the burner.

The whistling stopped, and for a moment she stood at the stove with her back to him.

Was she regretting the impulse? Was she wishing she hadn't done anything?

Then she turned around and her smile warmed his heart and soul.

"So now what, Cody Jameson?" she asked.

He pushed his chair back and was about to walk toward her, maybe get another kiss, when the door of the kitchen burst open.

"Vivienne, can you help me with this problem?" Bonnie called out.

Then she looked up and saw Cody. She frowned, glanced toward Vivienne then back to him while he hoped and prayed that it wasn't obvious what had just happened.

"Hey, Cody. You just get back?" Bonnie asked.

"Yeah. Vivienne saved supper for me." At least he didn't sound as disconcerted as he felt. And he hoped the momentary resentment he felt at his sister's inopportune arrival didn't show.

"Nice. You busy? Can you help me with my math, Cody?"

Cody was about to protest when Vivienne walked over to his sister. "Here, I'll help you with it. Cody's tired."

"Okay." Bonnie dropped the book down on the little table with a thunk and then frowned and bent over and picked up a gold hoop. "Hey, Vivienne. Did you lose an earring?"

Cody took a step away. "I gotta check on the horses," he mumbled and left before Bonnie could see the flush working its way up his neck.

Vivienne lay in her bed, staring up at the ceiling, her heart still beating out a heavy rhythm in time to the words running through her head like a refrain.

Cody kissed me. Cody kissed me.

She shifted to her side, staring at the rivulets of water trickling down the panes of the window.

Cody kissed me. Cody kissed me.

And she had kissed him back.

Now what? She blew out a sigh, her arms folded over her chest. For the past two hours she'd been lying here, her head a whirl of thoughts and worries. What about her future plans? She'd wanted to be a chef for so long. She couldn't abandon that dream because of a kiss.

It was more than a kiss.

The accusing words echoed in her head, and she couldn't dismiss them. But what was she supposed to do about this mixture of feelings roiling through her mind? Her heart?

She flipped onto her side, fluffed her pillow, rearranged herself and took another deep breath. And another. Time to sleep. Tomorrow was another day. Tomorrow she would see things differently.

An hour later, Vivienne's eyes were still wide open, her mind a snarl of confusion and worries as she stared into the absolute darkness of her room. Finally she gave up on sleep, sat up and clicked on the lamp on her bedside table. Golden light flooded the room, warming the wooden walls and chasing away the tangling thoughts and concerns.

She sat up and her eyes fell on the Bible sitting on the table by the lamp. She picked it up, fingering the worn edge. Her mother had given her this Bible as a birthday gift after her father died. In those horrible months after his death, she'd read every night. Then, slowly, as she, Zach and Brooke became accustomed to his absence, she read it less. In Paris and New York? Not at all.

But it had still come with her everywhere she went.

Now she opened the Bible, turning to the passage the pastor had preached on last Sunday.

"Trust in the Lord with all your heart and lean not on your own understanding. In all your ways submit to him and he will make your paths straight."

Vivienne let the words settle into her mind. Right now her paths seemed anything but straight. Too many maybes. Too many things out of her control. She'd made plans around her potential inheritance, but if Mei and Lucas didn't show up, all her work here would be for nothing.

And yet…

Her hand came up to her mouth, as if seeking evidence of Cody's kiss. So much had shifted in that intimate moment, but was she ready to go down that road?

She reread the passage, remembering the relief she had felt when she thought of releasing her problems to the Lord, as the pastor had encouraged them to do. Reminding them that the things this earth promised were fleeting and empty.

She repressed a flutter of panic at the thought of letting go of her plans. It seemed like she'd be letting go of herself. How often had her mother reminded her to take care of herself? Had those warnings so taken over her life that she was blind to other possibilities?

She covered her face with her hands, drew in a cleansing breath and prayed, her voice a thin sound in the emptiness of her cabin. "Please, Lord, help me to trust in you. Help me not to lean on my own understanding. Help me to know what I'm supposed to do."

She waited a moment, as if giving the prayer time to make its way to God, then she continued. "And please be with Lucas. Keep him safe wherever he is. And be with Mei..." Another flutter of panic followed that half-finished petition. Mei was a bit of a wild card. She always said she didn't feel like a true Clayton. Would it matter to Vivienne if Mei decided not to come?

Then, a realization came crashing into Vivienne's mind. Should it matter to anyone? If Mei didn't come and none of them got the inheritance, would their lives be worse for it? Should the money matter that much to any of them? Shouldn't their concern be more for Mei herself than what her presence meant financially to any of them?

She looked back at the Bible passage. "Trust in the Lord."

The ragged edges of her worry eased as the words soothed her concerns. "Trust in the Lord." After all, as she had known since she was a little girl, the Lord was her shepherd. She would not want. And for now, she was with her family.

And there was Cody.

She covered her face, praying once again for her family, for the people on the ranch and then, toward the end, for wisdom for herself and for peace for Cody.

Chapter Ten

The next day dawned bright and sunny. As Vivienne walked from her cabin to the cookhouse, she saw the mountains, snowcapped and towering over the ranch, as if protecting it. The moisture that had been rain down in the valley had been snow up high, and the peaks glistened pristine white.

She stopped a moment, enjoying the play of light on the rocks and snow, the intriguing shadows they created on the mountain's crags and valleys.

"You're looking chipper today."

The deep voice behind her made her jump. *Be calm,* she told herself. *Be levelheaded.* Then she turned.

Cody walked toward her, the smile on his face making nonsense of her moment of composure. Her answering smile almost hurt her cheeks.

"Nice day today," she said, reaching for the ordinary, the inane.

He didn't stop until he was right in front of her. His face only inches from hers. His hazel eyes were warm, and his smile raised a whisper of hope inside her.

"Wonderful day." Then he moved past her, but not before he caught her hand in his and gave it a gentle squeeze that sent her heart fluttering as quickly as his kiss had yesterday.

When she brought breakfast out, he had a secret smile just for her. Afterward, he came to the kitchen to thank her, then he stayed an extra few minutes, just chatting.

When he left, she felt as if the day had just lost some sparkle. She knew she wouldn't see him again until suppertime. So she got her work done for the morning and then grabbed her coat and pulled on her boots. As she zipped them up, she pulled a face. If she was going to do this walking thing more often, she would need better boots than these heeled ones. As she headed out the door, she promised herself that she'd buy some proper hiking boots soon.

"Vivienne. Vivienne."

The voice calling her name stopped her. Cody? She turned and there he was, walking toward her, his hat pushed back on his head, his welcoming smile softening his face.

"I thought you and the guys had to fix fences today?" She kept her question light, not daring to delve into why he was hanging around the ranch and not working as hard as he had been the last few weeks. She zipped up her coat and turned up the collar. In spite of the sun, a fall chill lacing the air hinted at winter.

"I've got enough men to delegate the work to," he said with a curious grin. "Besides, as Uncle Ted said, there's got to be some perks to being the boss, and today I'm just taking advantage of that." He angled his chin at her coat. "Where you going for your walk today?"

"No place special." She didn't want to admit to him that her initial plan was to head out toward the pasture. To watch the men—and Cody—working on the fences. She wasn't sure where they were, but she was willing to spend some time trying to find them.

Now he had found her.

"Have you been up to the waterfalls?" he asked. She shook her head.

"You have to see them," he said, putting his hand on her shoulder and giving it a gentle nudge in the opposite direction of the pasture. "We'll go down this path. It's a bit of a hike uphill." He glanced down at her boots and frowned. "You want to change?"

"I'll be okay," she said, not willing to admit

to him that this was all she had other than high-heeled shoes or the flats she wore when she was cooking. "I've walked in these before."

"Okay," he said, as if he didn't believe her. Which made her all the more determined to show him she could. He started walking and she followed.

While they walked he pointed out an unusual outcropping of rock, the way the trees changed and how the air got cooler.

She responded with a few comments, but because the walk was mostly uphill it took all her energy to focus on breathing and making sure she didn't twist her ankle in these silly city boots.

Twenty minutes later, her feet were burning, her arches ached, but the growing sound of rushing water helped her to push on.

"We're just about there," Cody said over his shoulder. Then he stepped off the path and pushed aside some spruce tree branches and stood to one side, indicating she had to go through. "Watch for the roots," he said, as she walked past him. "It's only a few more feet."

She followed the barely discernible path, taking careful steps with throbbing feet, but then the trees disappeared and so did her breath.

A huge chasm yawned in front of them, damp and rocky.

To her right, a silver stream of water dropped over fifty feet, tumbling and splashing over boulders and rocks into the creek at the bottom of the cut in the rocks. A gentle mist roiled up from the creek, creating an ethereal view of the trees clinging to the cliffs across from them.

A wave of dizziness washed over her at the depth of the gorge, and she reached to grab a tree. However, the only thing she caught was Cody's arm. He steadied her, then slipped his arm around her shoulder.

"So, was this worth the walk?"

Thankful for his support, she looked back at the view in front of her, overcome by the rugged beauty and the space yawning below her.

She drew in a steadying breath and shook her head. "It's amazing. I didn't know this waterfall was on the ranch."

"There's two more. They're higher up, but this one is the closest to the yard." His voice was a rumble against her side, and she found herself wanting to lean into him. To rest against him, to let him hold her up.

She hadn't felt that way around a man for so long, it left her feeling breathless and unsure.

You need to take care of yourself. Don't count on a man to take care of you.

The lesson her mother drilled into her head

wasn't easily forgotten. Vivienne knew this was a lesson her mother, widowed and left with three children, knew all too well.

Her mind slipped back to Darlene and Macy. Another woman left alone by a man to raise her child. Just like her sister, Brooke, when her boyfriend abandoned her. Just like her own boyfriend who had walked out of her life because they were on "different levels."

And yet the lonely part of her wanted to believe that men could be counted on. Didn't Cody look after his sister? Wasn't he an example of faithful love?

She turned her head to look at him, unnerved when she caught him looking directly at her.

"What is going on behind those beautiful blue eyes," he asked quietly, his hat shading the sun for her, as well.

His flirtatious comment sent her heart into overdrive. She didn't think he was the kind to indulge in flattery.

"I just…I think this is a beautiful place." It was all she could manage. Cody's nearness and the intensity of his gaze stole her breath and coherence. She dragged her attention back to the waterfall. "Thank you so much for showing me this."

He slipped his other arm around her so she rested completely against him, his arms warm across her stomach, creating a shelter. "To be honest, I had another reason for bringing you here."

She stood perfectly still, feeling like a feather floating on a delicate breeze above the chasm. One move in the wrong direction and she could either plunge into the foaming waters below or come to rest on the grass beside her.

So she said nothing, waiting.

"I wanted you to love this place as much as I do," he said. "I want you to be able to see the beauty of the ranch in all its forms."

She released her breath and laid her head back against his chest. "I do love this place," she admitted. "It's like every day I see something else to appreciate and enjoy. I can see why it's so much a part of you."

His chest lifted in a sigh. "I'm glad."

She let the moment settle, wondering what the repercussions of her words would be, then gently pulled away. "I should be getting back." She shot him a coy glance. "After all, I don't want to get into trouble with the boss."

He laughed at that. "I wouldn't worry about him. He's not as miserable as he looks."

"I know that," she said, and then before she could catch his reaction, she turned and walked back toward the path.

Only her feet, now swollen from not moving, were clumsy and stiff. Her boots, with their high heels, made it even harder to keep her balance. She took a step, turned her ankle and tripped over one of the roots Cody had specifically warned her about.

She stumbled, reached for a tree branch, caught it, but it wasn't enough to halt her forward momentum. She landed on her shoulder on the ground, twisting her foot in the process.

"Vivienne!" She heard Cody cry out, and then he was beside her, turning her over. She pushed his hands away, embarrassed.

"I'm okay. I just tripped. Like you told me not to." She tried to laugh as she got up. Pain shot up her leg and she stumbled again. She would have fallen, but Cody was right beside her.

He held her up as she grimaced and tried to put weight on her one foot.

"You hurt yourself," he said, his frown furrowing his forehead.

"Not really." But she knew she was lying through her clenched teeth. Her foot throbbed in time to her heartbeat, each pulse sending a shot of pain up her ankle.

"We need to get you back to the ranch." He heaved a sigh, looking down the path they had come up.

"What will you do? Carry me down?" she said with another feeble attempt at humor.

"Actually, yeah." He turned and bent his knees. "Get on. I'll piggyback you down the hill."

"I can walk."

Cody shot her a warning glance over his shoulder that she knew she'd better not argue with. At the same time, in spite of her tough talk, she knew she wouldn't make it down the mountain on her own, even if she took her boots off and walked in her stocking feet. So she swallowed her last bit of pride and got on Cody's back. He tucked her knees over his elbows and got up.

"Been eating too much of my own cooking," she said by way of apology.

"You hardly weigh a thing," he grunted as he shifted her weight and started walking. Branches slapped at her face as he plunged down the hill, and she struggled not to be too aware of the arms holding her or the shoulders supporting her.

"So your parents are missionaries and yet you ended up a rancher. How does that work?" she asked, trying to distract herself by making conversation.

"My mom and dad would send me to live with Uncle Ted, just like they are doing with Bonnie, from time to time, depending on where they were stationed," Cody said, his voice only a little more breathless than it had been on the trip up. Carrying her didn't seem to affect him much. "When I was ten I wanted to stay on the ranch full-time. Uncle Ted has only his daughter, Karlee, who didn't want to have anything to do with the ranch, so I started working with Uncle Ted and worked my way into buying half of his share."

"So you've lived here most of your life?" She clasped her hands tighter together, trying not to slip. She had been chilled when she got to the waterfall, but now the warmth from Cody's back seeped into her core and warmed her up, as well.

"Pretty much. I've been blessed to be able to do this. It's a big commitment, but it's all I've ever wanted to do."

Cody grunted as he took a large step down, wobbling on his feet a moment, then catching his balance again.

"I can try walking," she suggested.

"Just hold on…I'm not that feeble." But while they walked, she kept talking, determined to maintain some distance as each step made her more aware of his warmth and his closeness. She talked about the weather, asked about the cows. How many they had and why they had to move them, but nothing distracted her from his presence. She found herself wanting to lay her head on his shoulder, to draw even closer to him.

A couple of times she was tempted to ask him

if he had ever brought his wife, Tabitha, up to see the falls, but she didn't really want to talk about her.

"So how long have you wanted to be a chef?" he asked her, shifting the conversation away from him.

"Since I was little. I remember my grandpa George coming over to visit us while my dad was still alive. My mom was so flustered she asked me to help her." Vivienne's mind slipped back to those happier days as she remembered that meal. One of the few times her grandfather had come to visit, and one of the few times that, when he did, her parents didn't fight with him.

"And how did that go?" he asked.

"Actually, Grandpa was very complimentary. In fact, he was the one who told me I should think about going to school. To become a chef. Told me I had a rare gift to make food taste superb." She shifted her weight and laughed. "Up until then I thought the only thing chefs did was flip burgers like Gerald and Jerome at the Cowboy Café. Grandpa George expanded my horizons that day."

"So he wasn't as miserable as people make him out to be."

"Oh, he wasn't a storybook grandfather by any means," Vivienne said, clasping her hands tighter around Cody's neck. "He wasn't much help to my mom after my father died, though he would come over from time to time to see how we were doing. Too busy running after the dollar." No sooner had she spoken the words than Vivienne regretted saying them. After all, what was she doing right now by sticking around Clayton?

"He was a pistol, that's for sure," Cody said. He took a careful step and then paused, catching his breath. "Though I heard he had a lot of regrets toward the end of his life."

"That's what Reverend West told me." Vivienne also thought of the video of Grandpa George they had watched after the funeral and how he had asked them to find one good memory of him.

Well, she had it. The memory of her grandfather's rare smile as he ate the soup she had cooked and the pie she had baked. And how he had told her he'd never, ever eaten anything so good in all his life.

"I'm sure the inheritance is his way of making up for a lot of things. Though I'm not sure what I'll do with five hundred acres of land once I'm done my year here. I guess I could sell it when I move."

She felt Cody stiffen, which made her think again about their kiss. And the implications of that.

Could she really walk away in a year?

Cody said nothing more after that, and then,

thankfully, they broke through the trees and were at the ranch. He carried her right to her cabin and eased her off his back.

"I'll be okay now," she said quietly, sensing his withdrawal, wondering if it came because of her comment about selling the land. "Thanks so much for showing me the falls and for, well, carrying me back down here."

Their eyes met again. Cody nodded, and for a moment she thought he was leaving.

But to her surprise, he helped her into the cabin and then, ignoring her protests, slipped her boot off her injured foot.

"I don't think you broke anything. Probably just strained your ankle," he said, holding up the heeled boot as if it was the culprit. Which it probably was.

Vivienne grew more and more uncomfortable, but she wasn't sure what to say. Apologize for talking about her plans for the future?

But were they still her plans? Was leaving Clayton really what she wanted to do?

As her mind slipped back and forth, she looked down at Cody's head, bent over her foot as he pulled her other boot off.

She wanted to reach out and touch his hair. Stroke it away from his face. Lift it up so he was looking at her.

She closed her eyes a moment, uncertainty

about her future battling her growing feelings for Cody Jameson. She had her plans.

Plans could change, though.

Cody set the boot aside and then shifted his weight back on his heels, then he glanced up at her again. His eyes held hers and an awareness trembled between them. She knew she couldn't just brush this off.

"Tomorrow we're going down the road to get the first batch of cows and move them home," he said. "It's an easy gather. Would you like to come?"

Vivienne blinked. This was not what she had expected to hear.

"I could put you on Tango, my horse. He's quiet. Gentle. You won't have to use your foot."

Vivienne held his gaze, and her second thoughts became a whirling vortex. He was too appealing. Too attractive.

Too much of a distraction.

Say no. Don't go.

But Vivienne couldn't formulate the words she knew she should speak. So, instead, she simply nodded.

His grin made all her second thoughts worthwhile.

"And don't you dare think about making supper tonight or breakfast tomorrow. You stay off your foot. I'll get Delores to whip something up.

Bonnie can help her." He angled her a warning glance, and the concern in his voice gave her a gentle shiver.

"Okay. I won't," she said.

"Then I'll see you tomorrow." He got up, his knees cracking as he did so, then without a backward glance he walked out of her cabin.

Vivienne waited until he was gone, then she dropped back on her bed, her sigh disturbing the dust motes dancing in the beam of sunlight above her.

Was she crazy agreeing to go with him tomorrow?

You will see him every day for the next year, she reminded herself.

Unless she got another job.

She pulled her throbbing feet up on the bed and curled onto her side, staring at the door that Cody had just left through, his voice still echoing in her head.

Just take it one day at a time, she reminded herself. *For now, it's fun and enjoyable.*

Just enjoy the moment. Let the future take care of itself.

"Just stay here. I'll be right back." Cody saluted her with his coiled rope, nudged his horse in the side and cantered off.

Vivienne eased her foot out of the stirrup and

gave it a tentative turn. Yesterday, after she hurt it, she had done as Cody told her to, thankful for the reprieve from work and from seeing Cody again.

She stayed off her feet and stayed in her cabin, praying and reading her Bible, looking for solace. Direction. Answers.

She didn't find them, but she was nourished and refreshed when she was done. Even more important, she felt as if she had been able to rationalize her emotions toward Cody.

She read another book but found herself drifting away from the story, her mind zeroing in on Cody each time.

This morning when he came to see if she was coming on the gather, all her feelings flooded back as soon as she opened the door and saw him standing on the verandah of her tiny porch, filling it with his presence.

And now she was here, spending time with Cody and watching him in his own element and enjoying every moment.

"Hold them back," Cody called out as his horse came nearer to where the cows stood in a bunch, bawling. "They're crowding the fence."

Vivienne leaned forward in the saddle, resting her hands on the horn as she watched him. Cody's movements were fluid, in synch with the horse, like they were one entity.

He sat easily in the saddle as his horse side-stepped, spun around, then cantered off again to catch another bunch of cattle heading back up the hills to the old pasture. He brought them back to the herd, now spreading out over the path ahead.

"Bryce, get your horse beside those lead cows," Cody called out. "Don't get in front of them."

Even from here, well behind the herd, Vivienne could see Bryce's curled lip. That boy had such an attitude, Vivienne was amazed Cody still kept him employed.

Dust roiled up from the hooves of the cattle as they headed along the road toward the ranch. The cows bellowed and the calves bawled and above that the hands whistled and urged, keeping them all together. The sun, thankfully, had lost its summer heat and shone down with benign warmth.

In spite of that, Vivienne had taken off her jacket an hour ago. Ted had helped her tie it to the back of her saddle.

When Vivienne had imagined today, she'd pictured a bucolic atmosphere. Cows ambling quietly down the road, accompanied by the cowboys on horseback.

Instead it had been an initial chaotic move with calves skittering off, cows trying to follow them and men calling and racing after them on horseback.

They'd been at it for over two hours now, and

finally they all seemed to be headed in the right
direction. Vivienne had stayed far back, knowing that if she tried to help, she would probably
cause a problem. Just like she had when she'd let
the horses out of the corral.

Though she knew she couldn't do anything, she
did feel useless and every bit a city girl.

"Keep the pressure on, but keep back from the
leader," Cody called out to Bryce as he rode up
toward him. Then Vivienne heard nothing else
above the bawling of the cows and the pounding of their hooves on the dirt road. But through
the dust the cows raised she saw Bryce jerk back
on the reins, then spin his horse around and head
to the back of the herd. Obviously demoted,
Vivienne thought, watching him as he galloped
his horse back to where she rode. He shot her
an angry look and then jerked his horse around
again.

Vivienne wanted to say something about how
he was treating his mount, but she didn't know
enough. So she kept quiet, though it bothered her.

Grady rode up to Cody and with a nod and a
quick conversation, Cody handed the responsibility over to him.

Then Cody turned his horse and cantered back
to where she rode, one hand on his thigh, the other
handling the reins with imperceptible motions. As
she watched him, his gaze flicked over the cattle,

back and forth as if studying their movements. Then, before he joined her, he looked up at the mountains above them.

His smile was a white slash against his dusty face. His coat was streaked with dirt and grime, as were his chaps. But his happiness and contentment showed Vivienne how much at home he was in this element.

This is where he belongs, she thought. *This is who he is.*

She knew that on one level, but watching him working with the cows and working with the men brought this part of him to vivid life.

For a moment she was jealous of how at one he was in his environment. Because, though she hardly dared admit it, he looked happier here than she had ever felt in any of the jobs she had done.

What did it take to enjoy your work so much?

She had always thought owning her own restaurant would give her the contentment and peace she'd been looking for since her father died and their family became fractured.

But now?

She wasn't so sure, and she didn't like the self-doubts dogging her lately. She didn't like thinking that the plans she had thought would solve her problems instead distracted her from them. That no matter where she went, this unspoken yearning would follow her.

"You're looking pensive," Cody said as he brought his horse up beside her.

His horse jigged a bit, lifting his feet as if he wanted to run again, but Cody reined him in without even looking over at him.

"You've been reading your thesaurus," she returned, trying to create a lighter tone.

"Word of the day," he said with a wink. "You doing okay? Your foot okay?"

"I'm doing fine, and so is my foot."

"I could get someone to drive you back to the ranch if you're too tired."

Vivienne waved his concerns off with a gloved hand, feeling bothered that he thought she wasn't capable of handling this.

Of course, herding cattle was entirely new and she was a bit stiff, but she certainly wasn't telling him that now. Instead she glanced over at the cattle now heading, with purpose, down the road. "For a while I didn't think you would gather them all up."

"They were a mite spooky today," he said, reining his horse in again. "I think they were just nervous, having to perform in front of a city girl."

There it was again. She knew he was teasing, but a small part of her was bothered that this was how he still saw her. City girl.

She angled him a wry look. "Oh, yeah. I'm sure that's what made them extra skittish today."

"Skittish? Is that *your* word of the day?"

"That and *cantankerous,* but I decided to go with *skittish,*" she replied. "A little more appropriate for the circumstances."

The sound of Cody's laughter made her feel like she might actually be funny. And it sent a little flutter of happiness curling around her heart, easing away her little pique over his other comments.

"Well, they seem less discombobulated," Cody said. "Word of the day last week," he added with a wink in Vivienne's direction.

She laughed again as Cody got his horse settled into a steady walk.

In the easy quiet that followed, Vivienne felt a sense of peace slip into the moment. The sunshine, the movement of the horse, Cody's presence beside her came together in one of those perfect junctures of events one wanted to hold close, capture and store away against those days when life wasn't as peaceful. Or as easy.

"Horse behaving for you?" Cody asked with a tilt of his head toward Tango.

"Perfect gentleman," Vivienne said. "I'm not a horse person, but he makes me look good."

Cody grinned. "You look pretty good anyway.

And you seem pretty comfortable with him. I would have never guessed you hadn't ridden before."

His compliment increased the flutter, as did the way his eyes glowed when he looked at her.

"I'm glad you came along. Means a lot to me," he said quietly, edging his horse closer.

Vivienne's heart lifted again as she caught his direct gaze. "I'm glad I came, too." She glanced down at the low boots she had borrowed from Delores. "Though I'm sure my Jimmy Choo knockoffs are sad they couldn't come along."

"Whatever that means," Cody said, but his smile belied his comment.

She looked up and was surprised to notice the herd had moved a considerable distance ahead of them. She and Cody rode alone far behind everyone else. Though they were outside and the sky arched above them in an expanse of blue and the valley they rode through swept away from them and up to the rugged mountains, she felt a curious sense of intimacy.

"How did you train your horse to do all that?" she asked, glancing at his horse, who now plodded along, head down, the picture of docility—a complete contrast to the alert and responsive animal she'd seen moments ago.

"Time. Lots of time. And practice. When things are quiet on the ranch, I take him out to the cattle and work them. Separate the calves. Move the cows around."

"Is that called cutting?"

Cody shot her a curious look. "How do you know about that?"

Vivienne lifted her shoulder in a shrug. "I talk to the guys a bit. Here and there." Actually, she had talked to Ted one afternoon when he was hanging around the ranch and she had come back from her walk. Ted had told her a few things she didn't know. Told her about Tabitha, which explained a few things for Vivienne.

"Yeah...it's called cutting. It's an important skill for a cow horse to learn." Cody reached over and patted his horse on the neck. "Coco here isn't as docile as Tango, but he's looking to be a real goer."

Vivienne drew in a long breath, glancing around the valley, a sense of peace drifting over her. "It's really beautiful here," she said. "I'm so glad you asked me to come."

Cody edged his horse closer. "I'm glad you came, too."

Then he reached over and covered her gloved hand with his. Leather came between them, yet she felt his touch as easily as if her hands had been bare.

She glanced over at him, but his eyes were shadowed by his hat. She leaned closer, as if to get a better look. He leaned, as well, and then their faces were mere inches apart, moving in time to the horses' slow walk. Cody brushed his knuckle over her cheek, she moved just a bit and once again their lips met in an awkward yet tender kiss.

Vivienne was the first to draw back, a welter of emotions surging through her.

This was silly.

Yet so right.

You're a city girl, not a ranch hand.

But for now, none of that mattered. For now she and Cody were riding along surrounded by the beauty of God's creation.

"I wish I could tell you how much this means," he said quietly, their legs rubbing against each other as their horses stayed close. "You coming out like this."

His smile plucked at the center of her heart, because in it she read more than happiness. She read contentment.

And strangely enough, she shared his emotion.

The scent of warm horseflesh and oiled leather combined with the dust from the cattle created its own ambience so foreign to anything she'd ever done before, yet bringing with it a serenity she'd never felt before. She looked up into Cody's eyes and found herself drifting, moving toward him again.

She pulled back, trying to shift back to reality.

Too many things were uncertain in her life right now. This thing with Cody…it couldn't happen.

Could it?

"Did Tabitha ever come riding with you?" The question popped out of a need to regain perspective. Cody had been married before. That was his reality.

And a part of her wanted to find out more about his first wife. To know whether it was loneliness that caused Cody to kiss her. Or something else she wasn't sure she wanted to identify just yet.

Cody shook his head. "She always said this wasn't her thing. She was a city girl. Still don't know why she married me."

Vivienne knew why. Cody was a good man. A good catch.

If you wanted to live out on the ranch.

"Maybe she hoped you would change," she said quietly, trying to rein her horse away from Cody's. But her horse stubbornly refused to move away.

"Maybe." Cody looked ahead now and his expression hardened. "She knew who and what I was when we got married. I just wish…"

His sentence trailed off, and Vivienne caught a flash of pain in his eyes.

"I'm sorry that you had to deal with her death," Vivienne said, touching his arm. "I'm sure that was hard."

Cody's shoulders lifted in a slow sigh. "It was. But so many other emotions got tangled in her death." He kept his eyes on the dust cloud of the herd of cows now far ahead of them. "She was running away when she was killed in that car accident. She was leaving me. I don't know if you knew that."

Vivienne didn't know what to say, so she opted for simply listening.

"She said she couldn't live out here. Couldn't handle the isolation of living in a small town. I should have guessed. She was a glamour girl who couldn't adjust. I guess it wasn't fair of me to hope she would change and fall in love with the ranch." He clenched his jaw against his spill of words and drew in another breath. "But she never did. Tabitha was forever complaining about the house and buying new furniture. I couldn't do anything to please her. Twice she left. Then she would come home and things would get better, but just for a bit…"

"Go on," she said softly when he took a long, shuddering breath and looked like he might not continue.

"One day she left me a long letter saying she couldn't stay here anymore. She didn't love me anymore and was moving back to Denver. Back to her wealthy parents' place, where she said she could be who she wanted to be." His words came out in a rapid-fire tirade, then he released a bitter laugh, as if he still couldn't believe what happened. "I wasn't going to follow her, and I didn't. If she wanted to leave, I had to let her." He shook his head, his gaze still on the road ahead, as if ashamed of his actions. "I had always told myself that if she wanted to come back she would. She had in the past. I was never running after her or any other woman."

Vivienne heard the edge in his voice and wondered if she was included in that pronouncement. If it had anything to do with him asking her out so long ago.

And her turning him down.

He clenched his jaw, clamping back any other words that might spill out. His horse, as if sensing his tension, flicked its ears and tossed its head. Cody settled him but still said nothing.

Vivienne felt there was more to the story.

"Was that when she died?" she asked, keeping her tone gentle, her words quiet.

Cody blew out his breath and nodded. "She drove on to Denver, but she didn't make it. Her car slid on the road. It was wet and I'd been after her to get new tires on the car. I didn't have time to do it. I should have."

"It wasn't your fault," Vivienne said, hearing the guilt in his voice. "She made her own choices."

"But if I had gone after her. Tried to convince her to come back to the ranch, then maybe—"

His hands clenched on the reins.

"Maybe what?" Vivienne gently prompted, trying to catch his eyes. "Maybe she would have stayed? But would she have stayed long? She might have left again."

Cody dragged his gloved hand over his face and released a bitter laugh.

"She might have." When he looked at her, Vivienne almost recoiled at the raw pain in his expression, the chill in his eyes. "But maybe she would have had the baby she was carrying. If I had gone after her, maybe I'd have a child now."

Chapter Eleven

The angry words slashed the quiet.

Vivienne's heart grew cold as the implications of what he said settled into her mind.

She clutched the reins, her heart plunging. "So she was expecting?"

"I found out from her parents. She hadn't even told me." The words came out heavy, weighted with his sorrow.

He stopped his horse and Vivienne stopped hers. Then she pulled off her gloves and cupped his face with her bare hand. His skin was smooth, warm. And when he turned to her she saw the broken longing in his gaze.

"I'm sorry, Cody. So sorry." The words were a tiny offering, as was her touch, but she couldn't stand by and watch him and not connect in some way. He looked so forlorn. So alone.

To her surprise, he covered her hand with his,

and his sad smile touched her soul. "I've never told anyone this before," he said. "Other than Tabitha's parents. You're the only one who knows."

Vivienne frowned at that. "Not your uncle, or your parents?"

He released a short laugh. "When I got married I think my parents were more excited about the possibility of becoming grandparents than they were about becoming in-laws." He leaned forward in his saddle, resting his forearms on the saddle horn as he stared straight ahead. "I couldn't figure out how to tell them."

"You should. They need to know."

"Now? After all this time?" He angled her a curious glance. "They didn't even know what they lost. Won't it bother them?"

"It might, but it can also help you," she said softly, fiddling with the ends of her reins. Her horse stamped its feet but stayed where it was. "A burden shared is a burden halved."

He caught his lower lip between his teeth, then he turned to her, his face still shadowed by the brim of his hat. "I guess." Then he gave her a rueful little smile. "Thanks for listening."

"Of course."

As she held his gaze, knowledge that she was one of the few people who knew about his loss altered their relationship. His moment of vulnerability had slipped into her heart and shifted, once again, her perception of him. It had also created a deeper connection between them.

And where was that going? What would she do about that?

The ever-present questions pulled her in so many directions, she couldn't think. She needed some space. Some distance.

And this time, when she pulled on Tango's reins, he responded. Tango shook his head but then thankfully moved away from Cody. She took a chance, nudged her horse in the side and he broke into a quick walk. Minutes later she was caught up to the herd.

She didn't look back once to see where Cody was.

"Jasmine really enjoyed her afternoon at the ranch a couple of days ago," Arabella said, wiping four-year-old Jessie's face and then tugging Julie's ponytail straight.

It was Thursday afternoon and she and Vivienne were finishing up a picnic in the park.

"Spending time with you made her even more inspired to go to culinary school after she and Cade are married, which I'm happy about." Arabella used her shoulder to push her long, brown hair away from her face, then started packing up the leftovers from the lunch she and Vivienne had shared with her triplets.

"I'd love to do it again, even if Cody says the ranch is not a retreat center." Vivienne added an ironic grin as she wiped Jamie's little fingers on a napkin.

"Arabella did say something about Cody's reaction to their makeovers. He didn't seem happy."

Vivienne let Jamie slide off her lap so she could join her sisters on the old swing set. "Cody was worried about his little sister. She's been making eyes at Bryce, the hand that works at the ranch."

Arabella frowned. "Bryce Anderson? Tall, slender kid? Wears his hair in a buzz cut? Hangs out with Les and Billy Dean?"

"Add to that major attitude and that would be about right." Vivienne stood up from the picnic table, shook the crumbs off her skirt and then helped her cousin clean up the remains of their picnic.

Today was Vivienne's day off, so she had brought Bonnie to school this morning and then dropped her car off at Art Krueger's mechanic shop. The brakes were still not working properly. She'd had to put up with some mouth from Billy Dean, who accused her of riding them too hard. He told her they wouldn't be ready for a couple more days, so she made arrangements to get a ride back to the ranch with Grady's wife, Delores, who had come into town to do some shopping, as well.

Then she walked across town to her cousin

Arabella's place, thankful her foot felt much better. She was at loose ends. Brooke was bringing Darlene to an appointment with a specialist and Vivienne desperately needed to talk to someone about her situation. About her changing feelings for Cody and her confusion about her plans.

Because the weather was so beautiful, Arabella had decided to have a picnic. Now the creaking of the old, unoiled swings sang across the park, accompanied by the occasional growl of a truck heading to either the Cowboy Café or the grocery store across the street.

"Still don't know how you do it," Vivienne said, glancing back at the three girls. "Take care of the triplets, working long hours, helping with the wedding—"

"And thanks for offering to cater that," Arabella cut in, her golden eyes warm with gratitude. "I can't imagine taking care of that."

"I can't either, not on top of all the other things you do."

"I break my life into small goals. Try not to look too far ahead."

Vivienne sighed. "Something I've been trying to do the past while."

Arabella pushed her hair back from her face again, her golden eyes holding Vivienne's. "Is something bothering you?"

Vivienne handed her cousin the last of the containers and bit her lip, her feelings still such a muddle she wasn't sure she could even articulate them.

"Why did you stay in Clayton?" Vivienne finally asked. "You had a chance to leave when Auntie Katrina—I mean, your mom—got into that fight with Grandpa George all those years ago. Was it just because of Harry?"

Arabella looked around the square, as if taking stock of the town they had both been born and raised in. "My ex was part of the reason, and goodness knows Mom has been trying hard enough lately to get me to leave. But Clayton was and is my home. My mom has tried again and again to talk me into moving away, but I never had big dreams of living anywhere else, or doing anything else like you did." Then she zeroed in on Vivienne. "Why do you ask?"

Vivienne picked up a plastic bag and pleated it between her fingers, struggling to articulate her concerns and her changing feelings for Cody Jameson. "All I ever wanted to do was leave Clayton, become a chef, and look how well that turned out. Turfed out of my job."

"You didn't get fired because you were a lousy chef," Arabella admonished her.

"But I made a huge mistake that could have been fatal. If that wedding guest had eaten that shellfish, he would have died. They had specifically requested no shellfish."

"How were you to know? You were only working with the menu your boss gave you. He never said anything about no shellfish."

"I should have double-checked. I should have done my homework. I should have—" Vivienne caught herself there, the self-recrimination rising up to accuse her once again. "Anyway, I'm trying to put that behind me. I still want to start up my own restaurant. At least, I did."

Arabella frowned and came to sit down on the wooden bench beside Vivienne, her full skirt settling around her. "Did? Are you changing your mind?"

Vivienne shrugged, her attention still on the plastic bag she was mutilating. "I don't know," she whispered. "Lately, it seems things are changing. My priorities, my goals." She looked up at her cousin, the emotions she'd experienced the past few days suddenly needing expression. "I'm growing more and more attracted to Cody Jameson."

"And who wouldn't?" Arabella said with ill-contained glee. "Didn't he used to like you in high school?"

Vivienne waved her cousin's comment aside, a thread of shame wending its way around her heart even as her cheeks warmed at the thought of Cody's schoolboy affection for her. "I kind of think he does again."

Arabella's eyes widened, and then she punched her cousin's shoulder. "Seriously? You and Cody Jameson?" she squealed.

A young couple pushing a baby carriage along the park glanced their way, and Vivienne clapped her hand over Arabella's mouth.

"Would you shush," Vivienne hissed, glancing around, hoping no one else heard. But as far as she could see, the two women chatting in front of the grocery store and the old cowboy ambling down the street toward the drugstore didn't seem to notice. And thankfully the triplets had moved from the swings and were now playing hide-and-seek around the gazebo, their happy voices floating back to them. "Gossip in this town spreads faster than honey on warm toast."

Arabella pulled Vivienne's hand away from her mouth but kept it pressed between her palms. "So you and Cody Jameson?" she whispered, bringing her head closer. "That would be so cool. First Brooke and Gabe, then Zach and Kylie, then me and Jonathan, now you and Cody. That would be like the old days, all of us back here in Clayton."

Vivienne wished she could control her cousin's excitement. But Arabella's enthusiasm was catching, and she found herself flushing as she let her mind slip ahead.

"We're not a couple," she insisted, keeping her own voice low. "It's just…well…he's kissed me a couple of times."

Arabella's golden-brown eyes positively glowed as she squeezed Vivienne's hands tight. "I hope you kissed him back."

Vivienne didn't answer. Didn't have to. Her flaming cheeks accused her.

Arabella eyes went wide. "Wow. You and Cody Jameson."

"Trouble is, I feel like things are moving too quickly and I don't know which way to jump. I've wanted to be a chef for so long. Grandpa Clayton was the one who encouraged me and so did my home-ec teacher." She sighed. "I did so well at Cordon Bleu, and if we get Grandpa Clayton's money I wanted to start my own restaurant, and yet…Cody…" Her voice trailed off as she spoke his name.

"You sound like you're trying to convince yourself more than me."

Vivienne blew out a sigh, her eyes flicking back to the girls. "I remember when I found out you were expecting," Vivienne said, pulling her hands free from Arabella's. "I was still in school, but I felt so far away in Paris. I felt so alone. And, I have to say, a bit jealous. I think there's always been a part of me that wants to be married. To belong to someone. But there's always been a part of me that wanted to be a chef."

"Why was that? What made you have that desire to be a chef?"

Vivienne let her mind slip back. "After Dad and Uncle Vern were killed in that car accident, things fell apart at home. Then, after a month of eating sandwiches and cereal, I took over the cooking. Mom was so grateful. Zach and Brooke were happy again. We started eating together, and for a while our family was a unit."

"Maybe you see food as a way of healing. Of bringing people together," Arabella said, putting her hand on Vivienne's arm. "I know for me, my baking became an escape. Thankfully, I didn't eat too much of it," she said with a light laugh.

A tiny spark began to smolder, a blink of revelation at Arabella's words. "So you think my cooking is an escape, as well?"

"Or maybe a way of controlling things. Not that you're a control freak or anything." Arabella patted her arm. "You've been on your own a long time, and not just after you graduated. I know your mom kind of pulled back from you kids, too, after your father died. My mom did the same. And I think you seem to put cooking and acceptance in the same category. You need to try to figure out why you think you need to be a chef. Once you get that figured out, it might give you some insight as to what you really want."

Arabella's words slipped past Vivienne's guard.

Could her cousin be right? Had she become a chef for different reasons than she had always thought? Could she let go of her plans and still be Vivienne?

"But I do think you should let Cody into your life," Arabella continued. "Let someone else support and help you. Cody is a great guy, and I know he'll make a fantastic husband. He was amazing with Tabitha and didn't deserve how she treated him, but he was still so good to her. He'd be even better to you. I just know it."

Arabella's defense of Cody kindled warmth and tenderness deep within her, adding yet another layer to her emotions for Cody.

"He is a great guy," she agreed, her voice quiet.

"Your cooking career is important, but not important enough to be your whole life," Arabella said. "But don't twist yourself into circles trying to figure out what you need to do. Just take things one day at a time. After all, when Jesus gave us the Lord's prayer, He told us to ask for our daily bread. Not our monthly or yearly bread. Just our daily bread. I know I had to learn to live like that after Harry left me with the girls."

Vivienne let Arabella's words wash over her and give her comfort. She saw the wisdom in it. And yet...

"Okay. So take it one day at a time. But every time I even catch a glimpse of Cody, I'm not sure what to say. What to do."

Arabella chuckled. "Listen to you. It's like you're back in junior high, talking about your latest crush."

Vivienne released a feeble laugh. "I know. But that's how I feel around him. I've had boyfriends before, but with him it's like I'm not sure what to do. The last time he kissed me I ran away. Except I did it on a horse." She looked at her cousin. "I haven't dared talk to him since and he told me he doesn't go chasing after women and never would. But I miss him. So how do I come back from that?"

"Then make a gesture. Do something special for him. Make a move on him," Arabella added with a mischievous grin.

Vivienne tapped her lips with her forefingers, thinking. Then it came to her. She turned to Arabella, full of excitement. "Bonnie told me his birthday is coming up. She told me because she didn't know what to get him. But I could make him a special dinner and Bonnie could help."

"There you go. The grand gesture." Arabella shot her a grin. "I could make the cake if you want."

"No. I want to take care of every part of it." She immediately started planning. Thinking.

And getting more excited about the idea. She was about to say something more when the sun reflecting off a windshield caught her attention. A deputy sheriff's car pulled up beside the park, and Vivienne and Arabella both got to their feet as Zach strode toward them, his hat pulled low over his face. Like he had bad news.

"What is it, Zach?" Arabella was the first to recover as he came near.

"I've heard from the private investigator we hired to find out about Lucas," he said, his words delivered in a harsh monotone. "A man fitting Lucas's description has kidnapped a child from the drug dealers we thought he was involved in down in Florida. The P.I. thinks they are after Lucas and the kid."

Shock tingled through Vivienne. "Where is Lucas now? And the child?"

The white lines bracketing Zach's lips weren't encouraging. "We don't know. I'm working with the Florida state police to form a plan that won't jeopardize Lucas or the boy. I don't know why Lucas hasn't taken the kid to the police. We believe he's hiding."

Vivienne's stomach flopped over. "Surely Lucas isn't involved with these drug dealers?"

Zach held up his hand as if to stop her agitation. "I don't believe for a second that he is. We have to trust he knows what he's doing."

"Does Mei know this? Surely she should be informed about her brother," Arabella said.

"I'll be calling her next. I just heard and was going to your place, Arabella, when I saw you girls sitting here," Zach said, tapping his fingers on the heavy leather of his utility belt. "I needed to tell you right away."

"Do you want me to call Mei?" Vivienne asked. "We used to be good friends. I think we had a connection."

Arabella put her hand on Vivienne's shoulder. "I think that would be best. She did always listen better to you than anyone else."

Vivienne nodded and then glanced at her watch. "I've got to get going. I promised Delores I'd meet her in a couple of minutes." She glanced at Zach. "I'll call Mei as soon as possible and let you know what she says."

Vivienne turned to Arabella. "And thanks for your advice about, well, you know. I'll have lots to think and pray about."

Zach's stance relaxed as he glanced from his sister to his cousin. "Advice about what?" Zach asked in a fake aggrieved tone. "If you were having troubles, why didn't you come to your big brother?"

Vivienne gave him a playful punch on his shoulder. "Girl stuff," she said with a wink and a quick hug for him. "You wouldn't be interested."

"I can be interested," he called out. "I can be sympathetic. Kylie told me I am sensitive."

"Bye now," Vivienne called out, tossing out a wave. But as she left, she peeked back, pleased to see Arabella and Zach waving to her, the triplets calling out to her and waving, as well.

Family, she thought, smiling as she walked away through the rustling leaves. Such a blessing.

And on the heels of that thought came thoughts of Cody. With her cousin's advice still echoing in her mind, she hurried her steps. Back to the ranch, where she had plans to make.

Why was he wasting his time? Again?

Cody looked up from the his plate, unable to keep from watching Vivienne as she brought in another plate of French toast. Of course she'd added her own twist to the breakfast. Cody couldn't figure out what she'd put in it, but he'd had two helpings already, it tasted so good.

Might have had more if he wasn't feeling so out of sorts.

She wore her hair up again today, in some kind

of fancy twist. She had dangly earrings on, a silky white blouse and a skirt.

And those silly high heels she kept insisting on wearing. Obviously her foot was better.

Almost like she was trying to remind him of who she was. A city girl who didn't really belong here. A city girl who, as soon as she got her grandpa's money, was leaving.

She laughed at something Ted said, teased Dover about almost falling off his horse the day of the gather, then she straightened and caught his gaze.

Just as quickly, she looked away.

"You're looking grumpy, boss." Bryce nudged Cody in the side as he finished off the last off his coffee.

Cody shot the young man an irritated glance, other grievances slipping into his mind. "Where were you yesterday? It wasn't your day off."

Bryce gave a laconic shrug but didn't hold his gaze. "Had to do some stuff in town."

"Stuff that was more important than helping Grady haul bales to the cows?"

"He said he didn't need my help."

"You certainly came in late enough," Cody groused. And the only reason he knew that was because he couldn't sleep last night himself. He'd heard Bryce come back, and when he got up to check, he saw lights still on in Vivienne's cabin yet. At midnight?

Cody heard Vivienne's laughter ring out again, and his head spun in her direction.

This morning, Vivienne had greeted everyone with a smile and a joke. Everyone except him.

Bonnie wanted to sleep in this morning, so he'd come to the cookhouse to eat rather than sit in a quiet house on his own.

At least that had been his reason when he'd stepped out the door this morning.

Two days ago, after he had kissed Vivienne at the gather, it seemed his entire world had slipped end over teakettle. He didn't know which way was up.

Shortly after that, she'd ridden away and virtually ignored him the rest of the day and evening. Which didn't help his confusion any.

Yesterday was her day off, and she left for town as soon as she'd finished making breakfast. Bonnie had been serving it up when he and Ted came into the bunkhouse.

When Vivienne came back from town she disappeared into her cabin. She came out to make supper, and then vamoosed again.

You could make the first move.

I don't chase after women, he reminded himself.

And he certainly wasn't chasing after Vivienne Clayton again.

The fact that she'd talked to everyone this morning except him made him channel his irritation onto Bryce. "Last I checked, Ted and I are your bosses. Not Grady. You could have helped sort the cows. You know this time of the year there's always lots to do."

Bryce forked a piece of toast off the heaping plate in front of him and shrugged. "Guess I should have been around."

His insincere apology rankled, but Cody's attention was drawn, once again, by the sound of Vivienne's laughter. He glanced her way, surprised to see her looking directly at him.

He wanted to smile at her. He wanted to get up, grab her, pull her into the kitchen and kiss her again.

Or at least ask her why she'd been avoiding him the past couple of days.

I don't chase after women.

But his little refrain sounded hollow, because he knew that in the past few days he'd done exactly that.

And where has that gotten you? She's ignoring you.

He was done making the first move.

Bryce elbowed him in the side. "She's pretty, ain't she?" he said.

Cody gave him a brusque nod.

"Too bad she's a Clayton."

Cody frowned, glancing toward his hired hand. "What do you mean by that?"

Bryce shrugged. "They're all just sticking around long enough to get their money. They ain't innersted in Clayton. Or the people. Just money hungry. Like their old man and like his old man." The last words came out in a spurt of anger.

"Why do say that? You don't know anything about Vivienne."

Bryce ducked his head and finished the last of his breakfast. "I know what Billy Dean told me. And Les."

Cody knew he shouldn't ask, but he couldn't stop himself. "What did they tell you?"

Bryce wiped his mouth and tossed his napkin on the plate. "Said that when Vivienne dropped her car off, she said she got the boss of the Circle C wrapped around her little finger. That she's outta this hick town faster than you can say quarter of a million dollars." Bryce pushed himself away from the table. "I think she's trouble, boss. I think you should fire her."

"Thanks for your input," Cody said dryly.

"Yeah, well, she might not get her money anyway. I hear her cousin Lucas, the last one, ain't coming back. So she might be leaving sooner than later."

Bryce grabbed his plate and left, his words leaving a trail of suspicion and nastiness.

Cody wished he hadn't asked Bryce's opinion. Yet, in spite of his knowing better, the boy's insidious words seeped into his brain, feeding the uncertainty he struggled with.

He chased the last of his breakfast with the dregs of his lukewarm coffee and pushed himself away from the table. But just as he did, Vivienne came by with a pot of coffee.

"Did…did you want some more?" she asked. She sounded breathless.

"No. I gotta head out." He didn't have to, but at the same time, he felt suddenly uncomfortable around her.

"I see." Her smile faded and he regretted his brusque tone.

"But I could take it with me." He held out his mug.

"Um…sure. Don't you want like a travel mug, or insulated mug or something like that? I have one I could get you." She waved a fluttery hand in the direction of the kitchen.

"Um. Sure. Yeah." He almost rolled his eyes. What was going on? Why couldn't he string together any kind of coherent sentence around this girl? He should just leave.

He tried to dismiss Bryce's words as he followed her to the kitchen, but he couldn't ignore the snickers trailing behind them.

Did his other workers think the same way Bryce did?

"You take sugar, right?" she asked, still carrying the coffeepot as she reached up to pull a mug out of the cupboard. She got her hands around it, but then it clattered to the floor.

Cody bent over to pick it up, just as she did, and then their faces were inches away.

She smelled like roses and some other peculiar scent that he guessed was one of her fancy perfumes. Her eyelashes were dark, framing her soft eyes.

Her lips glistened.

And in spite of her avoiding him, all he wanted to do was kiss her.

Please, Lord, he prayed, *help me from making another stupid mistake.*

He had too much at stake. Bonnie depended on him. His hands and his partner needed him to make good choices and to keep his head on straight. It took him too long to recuperate from Tabitha. And Vivienne seemed to be blowing hot and cold. As if she were toying with him.

Got the boss of the Circle C wrapped around her finger.

He couldn't do this again.

And yet, as their eyes met, he couldn't stop

himself from reaching up and touching her face, letting his fingers trail down her soft cheek.

She caught his hand, and a smile softened her features.

Then, to his amazement, she leaned forward and brushed her lips over his cheek. Her lips were warm, soft, and their touch was like velvet. Then she straightened and spun away, not looking at him as she poured the coffee.

She spilled a bit, wiped it up and then handed it to him with an apologetic smile. "Here you go."

He nodded his thanks as he took the cup, feeling foolish. He felt like she was spinning him in circles, and he wasn't sure what to think of it all. He took a step backward to leave when she opened her mouth as if to speak again. Then she shook her head as she twisted the towel she was holding.

"You wanted to say something?" he asked.

"I was hoping I could ask you for tomorrow and the day after off," she said, not meeting his eyes.

He frowned. "But you went to town yesterday."

She nervously fiddled with a strand of hair that had come loose from her ponytail. "I know. But I need to go away for a couple of days. And I was hoping I could borrow a truck. I just need to get to the auto shop to pick up my car. I can leave the truck at Krueger's if that's okay."

He wanted to ask why she wanted to leave but

figured he didn't need to know. Maybe didn't want to know. "Sure. If you really need to. I think we can manage the cooking. And you can take my truck." He kept his eyes on her, but she still didn't look his way. Just kept twirling her hair around her finger.

"That's not necessary. I can take the ranch truck."

Cody waved off her suggestion. "You don't want do that. It's too dirty for you."

"I'm not that fussy," she protested, shooting a glance his way. "I can wear…something else."

He glanced at the clothes she had on, and she blushed as she fussed with the tie of her blouse. "I don't always dress up like this."

He frowned. "So why did you today?"

She opened her mouth as if to say something, then gave a shrug.

Had she dressed up for him?

He hardly dared believe that and was about to ask her if that was true when the door behind him slammed open.

"Cody. You gotta come out right now," Grady called out, breathless. "The cows are all over the yard."

Cody's heart jumped in his chest. Stupid cows and their lousy timing.

"Sorry. Gotta go," he muttered in Vivienne's direction, dropping his hat on his head. He took a few steps backward, though, still looking at her.

Their eyes met, and in that moment he felt it. That connection of something shared. Something deeper than attraction. He wanted to stay. To talk to her. Maybe even steal another kiss.

But he had work to do. "I'll talk to you later."

Then he turned and ran out of the kitchen to deal with this new disaster.

As the door slammed shut behind Cody, Vivienne leaned back against the counter, her hand resting on her chest.

And wasn't that a scintillating conversation?

She shook her head at her own foolish meanderings.

Yesterday when she'd come back to the Circle C, she felt as if her talk with Arabella had made everything between her and Cody more real and immediate. It made her nervous, excited and wound up. The thought of facing him made her blush and overly self-conscious. So she retreated into her cabin and started planning his birthday dinner as a way of escape. Then she read her Bible and tried to lay everything—her feelings, her future and her plans—in God's hands.

This morning, knowing she couldn't avoid Cody any longer, she'd spent almost an hour picking out her clothes, doing her hair and makeup. All in the hopes of catching Cody's attention.

But he took forever to come into the cookhouse, making her think he wouldn't show up at all.

When he finally made an appearance, she'd gotten herself into such a frazzle, she couldn't think.

She had hoped to thank him for taking her out riding the other day. And from there, she'd hoped to have a simple conversation with him. As she turned back to the mound of dirty dishes needing her attention, her mind wandered back to that kiss she stole, and she blushed again.

What was she thinking? How could she have been so bold? She blamed her reaction to him on her silly move. He made her feel all giddy and flustered, that was all.

Her cheeks burned as she thought of the kiss, but behind that came the memory of his finger trailing down her cheek.

What was happening between them?

Was she trying too hard to analyze and take apart? Was she trying to stay in control?

Please, Lord, she prayed, *help me, like Arabella said, to just pray for what I need for today.*

And in spite of Arabella's advice, she added, *And help me to know what I should do for the future.*

Chapter Twelve

"So is this where the cows got out?" Ted asked as he got off his horse, leading it to where Cody and Bryce were working on a gap in the fence.

"From the tracks in the ground, I'd say yeah. Not even that far from the yard. I can't believe they didn't get out sooner." Cody hammered another staple into the fence post. "Pull that wire tighter," he told Bryce.

"Can't figure why those cows would put that much pressure on a barbed-wire fence," Ted said.

Cody shot an annoyed glance at Bryce, who was supposed to be helping him but wasn't paying attention. "Tighter, Bryce. Reef on that puller, would you?" He restrained his annoyance with the young boy, putting it down to a number of factors.

His anger when he found the fence cut.

And his growing confusion with Vivienne. One

moment she seemed to ignore him, the next she was kissing him. One minute she was all city girl and perfume and pretty hair, the next she was sitting on a horse and letting him kiss her, then she was taking off and ignoring him.

Wrapped around her little finger.

He knew he cared for her more than he dared admit. And he also knew this was a dangerous proposition. In spite of the malice in Bryce's tone this morning, he was only voicing something Cody knew for himself.

Vivienne wasn't here for the long haul. She'd made that pretty clear again and again.

And yet…

He glanced over at the cookhouse, where he knew she was busy, getting something ready for supper tonight so she could leave.

"The cows didn't pressure the fence," Cody said, pulling another staple out of the bucket at his feet. "Someone cut it."

"Cut the fence? Why would someone do this? And when did this happen?" Ted's rapid-fire questions resurrected the anger Cody felt when he found the clipped wires. It wasn't too difficult to see they'd been cut.

"Last night, far as I can tell from the footprints by the fence," Cody grunted as he hammered the staple onto the taut wire. He and the men had spent the whole morning rounding up the cows and all afternoon fixing the fences they had ruined in the rodeo that followed. They were doing the last bit of fence close to the main yard and were almost done.

Cody straightened, easing a kink out of his back. "When the cows got out they didn't show up on the yard until they got hungry and headed for the bales this morning."

"Do you have any idea who did this?" Ted asked, slapping his gloves against his thigh. "Can't believe someone would cut our fence."

Bryce cleared his throat. "Well, if it's any help, I saw Cade hanging around late last night. I asked him what he was doing. He said nothing. Thought it was weird."

Cody shot his hand a puzzled look. "When was this?"

"Just before I went to bed. Then, this morning the cows were out."

Anger surged through Cody, but it was followed by uncertainty. He remembered the night he came back from finding that cow. Cade had been hanging around then, as well. What was he doing then?

He quashed the uncertainties, reminding himself that Cade may be a son of Charley Clayton, that no-good layabout, but Cody was sure he was a decent kid. Didn't make sense that he would do something like this. "Where is Cade, by the way?"

"He went to fill out some forms for going to college," Ted pushed his hat back on his head, leaning on a fence post. "You don't need to do this, Cody," he said. "Let Bryce finish up. You go talk to Vivienne."

Cody shot his uncle a puzzled glance, but when he caught his uncle's eye, he realized what Ted was up to. Ted may be hard of hearing and maybe he was slower getting on and off his horse, but his wits were sharp and his keen eyes didn't miss much.

Cody was pretty sure his uncle had an idea of his feelings toward Vivienne.

"That's okay. I want to oversee this myself."

Trouble was, he didn't entirely trust Bryce to do the work properly, and the other hands were either checking the herd or riding out, making sure all the cattle were accounted for.

He picked up his bucket, and as he walked to the next post a movement caught his attention.

Vivienne had come out of the cookhouse, her purse in one hand, a leather briefcase in the other, a coat over her arm. She still wore her skirt and shirt and fancy high heels.

Heading off to town again. Just like Tabitha always did.

She's not the same. She isn't. She's only gone for a few days and she's coming back.

So why is she going to town again when she

went yesterday? And why is she staying away a couple of days?

She kissed you this morning.

And now she's going.

A chilly wind blew across the yard and Vivienne slipped the long coat on, then picked her way toward where they were working.

In spite of the chill in the air, a trickle of sweat worked through the grime on his face, on its way down Cody's temple. His coat was dusty and his blue jeans caked with dirt from working the cattle back into the pasture all morning and fixing fences all afternoon.

His grubby clothes and dusty face were a complete contrast to Vivienne in her white coat, bright red shoes and shining hair.

He straightened as she came closer, hoping this time he could keep his reaction to her under control.

She gave him a dazzling smile, and his stupid heart jumped up against his ribs so hard he was surprised his uncle and Bryce didn't hear it.

"Hey there, Cody," she said, her voice holding that husky tone that sent goose bumps down his spine. "So, is it still okay to take one of the trucks this weekend?"

He shifted the pail of staples from one hand to the other, overly conscious of how scruffy he looked. "Take my truck. It's all fueled up and the keys are in the ignition." He had made sure one of the guys got it ready. Just in case.

She frowned. "Are you sure? I'm gone a couple of days."

He wanted to ask where she was going and why, but fear simmered below his unspoken questions. His feelings for her were changing a lot, but he still harbored doubts and concerns.

"It's okay."

She looked past him to the fence he'd been working on. "So you got the cows all back in? How did they get out?"

"Someone cut the fence."

"What? Why would anyone do that?"

Cody shrugged. "Don't know. I hope we find whoever did it. Caused me a lot of trouble and time."

Uncle Ted cleared his throat and Cody shot him a frown, wondering what he wanted.

"I want to take Bryce over to the tack shed. I need him to help me fix my saddle."

"You should get a new one," Cody said absently, his attention on Vivienne.

"I might. I know of a guy north of here who has one for sale. But for now Bryce and I can work on this one." Ted caught the boy by his arm and led him and his horse away.

Then Cody and Vivienne were alone. He took a step closer, his doubts fading in her presence. She seemed glad to see him and happy to be around him.

"Breakfast was really good this morning," he said quietly. "I really enjoyed it."

"Thank you." She fidgeted with her briefcase as if she wanted to get going.

"Um, so you make sure you drive safely, okay?"

"I will."

"Where are you going?" The question slipped out before he could stop it. He wasn't going to ask, but he had to know.

She pressed her lips together and looked away, as if she didn't want to tell him, and immediately he was sorry he asked.

"Actually, I need to go to Denver," she said. "I have a good friend there…" Her words faded away and her hesitancy raised all the questions he thought he'd dealt with. "I hope that's okay," she said, still not looking at him. "I know when I asked for the truck, I never told you where I was going."

"None of my business, really," he said, hoping he sounded more casual than he felt. He wanted to ask why but kept his questions to himself.

But at the same time, he couldn't let her leave like this. He let go of his pride and the pail, took a step closer and brushed a kiss over her lips. "Make sure you come back safely," he murmured.

Her startled look made him wonder if he had done the right thing or if he had said too much. But in spite of his confusion, he needed her to know that he wanted her to come back. That he'd be waiting.

She gave him a tentative smile, then walked away without another word. Just before she got into the truck, she turned and waved at him.

Then she drove away.

Cody waited until she was out of the driveway, fighting down an eerie sense of déjà vu. The day Tabitha died, he watched her drive away, as well.

It's not the same, he told himself. Vivienne wasn't leaving. She was just going on a short trip.

Please, Lord, watch over her, Cody prayed, as the truck made the last turn in the bend. *Please bring her back.*

It was all he could do.

Because deep in his heart, he knew what he felt for Vivienne was different than what he ever felt for Tabitha. His feelings for Vivienne were deeper, more profound. They fit together in a way he never felt with Tabitha.

And Vivienne had the potential to hurt him more deeply than Tabitha ever did.

"Whatcha got cookin'?" Bryce strolled into the kitchen, his hands in the pockets of his down jacket. "Smells good."

Vivienne looked up from the soup she was stirring, frowning at the young man. "What can I do for you?" she asked, putting the lid back on the pot with a clang. She had been back from her trip to Denver a few hours already but hadn't seen Cody yet. Though she was disappointed, his absence was a good thing because she could work on Cody's surprise birthday dinner.

"Just thought I'd let you know I gave Cody your message when you called the other day from Denver."

"Why are you telling me this now? I gave you that message a couple of days ago."

Vivienne had planned on coming back to the ranch Sunday but her girlfriend had a medical emergency and no vehicle, so Vivienne brought her to the hospital. Then she stayed an extra day just to make sure she was okay. She had called the ranch to ask if she could have the truck another day, but Bryce answered the phone. So she asked him to pass the message on to Cody.

"Just thought I'd let you know."

"Okay. Thank you," Vivienne said, distracted by all the work she had to do yet. She knew she had cut things close by coming home today, but she still had time.

Bryce shifted closer to her, then lowered his voice. "Thought you should know somethin' else," he said quietly. "You know that cut fence from the

other night? When the cows got out? Know what
we found there?"

"I have no idea," she said, giving the soup another stir, adding a smidgen of salt.

"Boot prints. Just like yours."

The insinuation sent a shiver of dread through
her. She lowered her knife, staring at Bryce.
"What are you saying?"

Bryce gave an exaggerated shrug, followed
by a smirk. "I'm saying Cody thinks you were
hanging around that fence that night it got cut.
Funny thing, huh?" His smirk grew and he shot
a glance past her to where Bonnie was working.
"Hey, Bonnie. You're looking good."

Bonnie blushed and Vivienne's heart grew cold.
She wanted to leave, get away from this little
weasel. He couldn't be telling the truth, could he?
But she left the day Cody was fixing the fence
and she hadn't talked to him since.

Bryce angled his chin toward the china sitting
out on the butcher-block counter. "You want me
to help you set the table?"

"No, thank you. Bonnie and I will do that." She
put the lid back on the pot and wiped her hands
on her apron, glancing over at Bonnie, who was
looking Bryce's way. "Bonnie, let's go."

She handed Cody's little sister a stack of plates,
took some dishes and cutlery out and headed out

of the kitchen, determined to get away from Bryce and his nasty insinuations.

Ted was in the dining room when they came out.

"When are we eating?" he asked.

"In an hour." Vivienne wiped her hands on her apron, glancing around. "Is Cody back yet?"

"Still gone, which don't make sense. He said he would pick up your car and come right back." He gave a shrug. "Maybe he had something else to do. But meantime, I'm gonna grab me a cookie."

Vivienne just shook her head. Ted had a terrible sweet tooth. She knew it would be more than a cookie he was helping himself to in the kitchen. As long as he stayed away from the desserts…

An hour later, candles flickered on every table, all covered with cloths that Vivienne had scrounged together. The places were all set, and everyone she had asked to come was waiting, but Cody still wasn't back from town.

Vivienne hovered, darting between the dining room, looking out the window to see if Cody was coming, then back to her slowly deteriorating birthday dinner.

Bryce came into the kitchen once to check on the progress of the food and announce that he was really hungry. One time Cade was sent in to check on things, as well.

An hour later, the soup was shrinking, the

salads were getting soggy, the potatoes were drying out and the people waiting for their dinner were starting to grumble. Cody still hadn't made an appearance or even phoned.

Vivienne stilled her own nervousness. She had tried a number of times to call his cell phone but was sent directly to his voice mail.

"I'm starving," Dover said, pressing his hand to his stomach when she came back into the dining room. "Can we eat now?"

Vivienne bit her lip, thinking. Sure it was supposed to be Cody's special dinner, but the meal was getting ruined the longer she waited.

She glanced at Bonnie, who simply shrugged, then Vivienne made a decision. "I guess we'll eat," she said, disappointment lacing her voice.

Vivienne started with the soup and then served the rest of the meal. Instead of sitting down, as she had figured she would, she brought the food out and cleared the plates, unable to eat, wondering where Cody was. Half an hour later, dessert was done and everyone was sitting around, complimenting her on the food, all complaining they had eaten too much.

"That soup had a unique flavor," Grady's wife said, wiping her mouth with her napkin. "I'd love to get the recipe."

"Good luck with that," Bryce said with a laugh,

then he coughed. "Though Cade might have an idea 'bout it."

Vivienne ignored his silly ramblings. "I can get you the recipe, no problem."

She got a few more compliments, which made her feel better, but as she cleaned up, disappointment dogged her every move. She had worked so hard to make Cody's birthday meal special, and he hadn't even been present.

Two hours later the stove gleamed, the countertops shone, the dishes were all put away and the only remnants of the meal was a bowl of soup and a plate of food she had saved for Cody to heat up in the microwave. She hadn't eaten a bite herself, blaming her lack of appetite on nerves.

Why didn't Cody come?

She was just finished wiping down the taps of the kitchen sink when Dover staggered into the kitchen.

"You got something for an upset stomach?" he asked, clutching his abdomen. "I feel terrible. I've been throwing up for the past hour."

"What?" Vivienne tossed the cloth into the sink and hurried over to Dover's side. His face was gray and his eyes red. "What happened?"

"Grady is feeling the same. So is his wife," Dover groaned, bending over. "I think something was wrong with the food."

Then, to Vivienne's horror, he collapsed onto the kitchen floor.

Cody ran a few more steps and then walked a few, clutching his side as he stumbled down the last bend in the road to the ranch. For the past two hours he'd been alternately running and walking and the stitch in his side grew worse and worse. He should have never taken that detour to pick up that saddle for his uncle. Uncle Ted had called him asking Cody to get the saddle because the buyer had someone else lined up, and if Cody didn't come right away it was gone.

So, after picking up Vivienne's car from the mechanic, Cody had reluctantly made the out-of-the-way trip to get the saddle. He would have been at the ranch two hours ago if he hadn't.

And Vivienne might have been the one driving her car, instead of Cody, when the brakes failed.

For ten terror-filled seconds, Cody had gone careening downhill, unable to stop. Thankfully he knew the road and had been able to turn off the road onto an uphill grade, which slowed the car enough for him to turn it into the ditch and stop it.

But he had ditched the car a two-hour's walk from the ranch.

He tried not to think of the time or how angry

he was at Art Krueger for not doing a better job on Vivienne's car.

Meantime, he hoped no one at the ranch was too worried about him. When he called the ranch he got Bryce on the phone, which seemed weird. Cody didn't bother asking Bryce what he was doing in the kitchen. He just told him he might be late, to pass the message on and then his phone died. Correction: Vivienne's phone died.

And the reason he was using Vivienne's phone was because she had left it in her car when she dropped it off at Art's. And he had been driving Vivienne's car back to the ranch because he thought he would surprise her and take it back to the ranch for her.

Good thing he did. First chance he got he was heading back into town to give Art Krueger a piece of his mind. He didn't even want to think what could have happened if Vivienne had been driving that car when the brakes failed.

He jogged a bit, then slowed down and walked again, his mind on Vivienne and what waited for him when he got to the ranch.

The entire way back, his mind shifted between anger with Art for what happened to Vivienne's car and the words of that chef from Denver. When Vivienne's phone rang, he'd answered it without thinking. And the person on the other end of the line was some guy named Chef Eduardo. From Au Gratin in Denver.

"Tell Vivienne I looked at her résumé and I'd be honored to have her come and work. Anytime. I'll make room for someone of her caliber," he had said, asking Cody to pass the message on.

Looked at her résumé.

Honored to have her come and work.

And as Cody agreed to pass the message on, fear and confusion clawed at his chest.

That's why she wanted to go to Denver. That's why she stayed a few more days and didn't tell him.

He pushed the traitorous thoughts down. He couldn't think that, not without talking to Vivienne first.

Then, finally, he rounded the last bend and saw the lights of the ranch. He took a shortcut through the trees, branches slapping at him. When he broke through into the clearing, it was to see a number of cars parked by the bunkhouse, another unfamiliar car by Grady and Delores's house and one by the cookhouse.

And more confusion slipped into his already busy mind. What was going on? What were these other vehicles doing here?

Lights blazed in every building. The cookhouse was closest, and as he ran toward it a door opened and light streamed out into the dark.

Then a figure emerged, silhouetted by the light behind him.

Cody frowned as the figure turned. Was that Jonathan Turner? What was a doctor doing here? Ignoring the pain in his side, Cody ran harder.

"What's going on?" he gasped as he made it to the door, pressing his hand against the wooden building to support himself.

"Where did you come from?" Jonathan shifted his bag to his other hand, frowning at Cody, who fought to suck in enough air. "Are you okay?"

Cody waved him off. "What's happening?"

Jonathan glanced over his shoulder, then back at Cody. "You got a number of sick hands. My diagnosis is food poisoning."

"Sick? Food poisoning? Again? How sick is everyone?"

"Whoever has it doesn't need to go to the hospital," Jonathan continued, his voice even and calm, smoothing away some of Cody's concern. "They'll need extra care. You weren't here, so Vivienne and I got the Church Care Committee coming tomorrow to help out."

Cody looked past Jonathan and saw Vivienne standing just beyond him. She leaned against the counter, her hand over her mouth, her other arm clasping her stomach.

"Are you okay?" His concern made him push past Jonathan. He caught Vivienne by the shoulders, relief flooding through him. She had come back after all. She was still here.

But her gaze was locked on the floor, wisps of loose hair falling over her cheeks.

"It's my fault," she said, her voice muffled by her hand. "They got sick from the food I gave them."

"What? I don't understand." He cupped her face in his hand, his mind playing catch-up as he tried to absorb what was going on. Tried to absorb the fact that she was still here. Still cooking for his men.

She looked at him, and Cody's heart dropped at the anguish in her eyes.

"I wanted to make a special supper for you." Her hands drifted sideways in a gesture of confusion. "But I messed up. Again. I'm useless. I'm no better than that other cook you hired—Stimpy."

"What are you saying?"

She just looked at him, pain in her eyes. She reached out, touched his face, then she lowered her hand.

"I can't be here," she whispered. "It's time for me to go."

Cody watched her face tighten, saw her fingers curl into fists. Watched her move away from him.

"I have to go," she said. "This isn't worth it. I have to leave."

Her beautiful face was full of anguish. But it

was the definite tone in her voice that chilled his heart. Her voice spoke of purpose. Of decision.

Looked at her résumé. Honored to have her come.

I have to leave.

She raised her chin, as if she had made up her mind. "Sorry, Cody," she said. "I have to go. Right now. I don't belong here."

Then she turned away from him, walking toward the back of the building.

He lowered his arms, his own resolve hardening as he watched her walk away.

Go after her. Find out what she means. Find out what's going on.

But the cold around his heart flowed into his veins.

No. He wasn't going after her. Not when she couldn't be bothered to tell him the truth about why she had gone to Denver.

He had promised himself he was never running after a woman again, and he wasn't starting with someone who couldn't be straightforward with him.

He shook his head and spun around on his heel. He stormed out of the cookhouse, not sure where he was going. Sure only of one thing.

He was done with Vivienne Clayton. She was a city girl and she was leaving. Going back to where she belonged.

Chapter Thirteen

"Are you feeling better?" Cody perched on the edge of his uncle's bed, his hands resting on his thighs. This was the first break he'd had in his work the past couple of days and the first chance he'd had to talk to his uncle since the food-poisoning incident.

Ted made a face, then pushed aside the bowl of soup he'd been working on for the past ten minutes. "I'd be feeling a lot better if I could be eating Vivienne's cooking 'stead of this slop."

"I'm sure Dorothy Henry would lash you with her lacy hanky for calling her soup slop." Cody attempted a feeble grin to go with his feeble joke, wishing his uncle's mention of Vivienne's name didn't start up the dull ache he'd been trying to suppress the past few days.

It was a mixed blessing that his men were sick. Meant he was busy from the minute he cracked his eyes open until the second he dropped, weary from exhaustion, into bed.

Cody had gone through the motions of work, doing what he could, keeping thoughts of Vivienne at bay.

Vivienne was a city girl. He should have known. He simply had to forget her.

So why couldn't he get rid of this ache in his chest? Why couldn't he move on like he did after Tabitha? Why did his life seem to stretch ahead of him empty, devoid of life?

Thankfully he still had his faith. He still knew that in all the ups and downs of his life, God was faithful.

And thankfully his men hadn't gotten sicker.

The people on the ranch were being taken care of, so at least he didn't have that on his mind. Every day someone else from the Church Care Committee came delivering meals and visiting with the people who were sick. Some offered to help Cody, but he politely declined, preferring to lose himself in the busyness of his work. Diving into exhaustion in the faint hope it would keep thoughts of Vivienne buried.

"You look like you could use some soup, even if it is slop," his uncle said, leaning back against the pillows.

Of everyone, Uncle Ted had been hit the hardest by the food poisoning. Cade was already up and about. He was checking on the cows right now, giving Cody his first break in two days of steady work, and Dover was helping him feed.

"I'm okay."

"No, you're not," Ted said, drilling his gaze into Cody's. "You look like someone shot your horse, rode over your dog and crashed your favorite truck."

Trouble was, all of the above was preferable to what he was feeling now.

"I'm just tired," Cody said, stifling a yawn.

"You get Vivienne's car back to Art's?"

Cody nodded. Zach had made sure a tow truck had come to bring the ditched car back to the mechanic's shop.

"I'm sorry I bugged you to get that saddle," Ted said, folding his hands over his chest. "You could've been here for Vivienne."

Cody shook his head. "I'm not sorry. If I hadn't picked up that saddle, Vivienne would have been driving her car when the brakes failed."

"Have you talked to Vivienne?"

Cody threw his uncle an annoyed look. "She's gone."

"You don't know that."

Why wouldn't she be gone? Great job offer from Chef Eduardo at Au whatever-the-name-of-that-restaurant-was. At any rate, she hadn't contacted him or even bothered to come back for her things. Her sister, Brooke, had done that one day while he was out working.

Bonnie had been moping around, as well, saying how much she missed Vivienne, telling Cody he was stupid to let her go. Bonnie didn't know he had had nothing to do with her leaving. Vivienne had left of her own free will. Gone off to Denver.

Cody pressed his hands to his knees and pushed himself to his feet. "Well, I better go see how Grady is doing. Now that Bryce is gone, things are even busier."

"I heard that little weasel quit."

"Yeah. He left the night everyone got sick." Cody dropped his hat back on his head and threaded his arms through the sleeves of his lined oilskin. "He didn't even have the decency to tell me to my face."

Ted stroked his grizzled chin, blinked a couple of times, then looked up at Cody. "Did Jonathan ever find out how we got the food poisoning?"

Cody shook his head. "He figured it was the soup, 'cause only the people who had the soup got sick."

"I don't suppose they did a test on that soup?"

"This isn't *CSI Circle C,* okay? No one died. They just got sick. We did the math, and that's what Jonathan came up with." Cody stifled his exasperation. He knew his temper was on a hair-trigger these days, and he knew why. It wasn't his uncle's fault, though. He drew in a long breath and prayed, once again, for patience. For strength to get through the next while. Because sooner or later memories of Vivienne would fade away. "It was just the soup and that's all. I just wish—" He captured the last angry words with clamped lips.

"What do you wish?"

Cody pushed away that question with a backhand. "So tell me what's flapping in your brain."

Ted simply nodded, then said, "I saw Bryce fiddling with that soup. Just before the dinner, I went in to get a cookie and I saw him stirring it." Ted pushed himself upright, his eyes growing bright. "He must have done something to the soup or put something in it. I asked him what he was doing and he said Vivienne asked him to make sure it wasn't burning. But Vivienne wouldn't let anyone touch her food, would she?"

This caught Cody's attention. "No. She wouldn't. Bonnie often complained that when Vivienne made dinner she would hang over everything she did, making sure Bonnie did it exactly right."

"And Vivienne and Bonnie were working in the dining hall when I went into the kitchen." Ted stabbed the air with his finger. "You go talk to that weasel. Find out what he did. Then tell Vivienne so she won't think she poisoned us."

"I'll pass the information onto Zach. He's the sheriff. He can deal with it."

Ted narrowed his eyes. "You need to tell her yourself. Poor girl is probably beating herself up over what happened. Probably wishing you would come. She cares about you. And any fool can see it, except you, apparently." He sighed wearily. "I'm sure she's wishing right now you would come and forgive her. Tell her that you still care."

Ted's words stung and at the same time raised the specter of false hope. "Vivienne is in Denver," he said, quashing his uncle's optimism. He wasn't going to say anything about still caring for Vivienne, because even acknowledging that hurt too much.

"How do you figure?"

"I got a call on her phone from some chef in Denver saying he looked at the résumé she dropped off when she was there a few days ago. He offered her a job. She's gone."

Ted's frown and subsequent head shake started a niggle of unease. "She wouldn't do that. She won't get her money that way."

"Before she left she said that no money was worth this. I think she's bugging out on the inheritance," Cody was saying as the door of the cabin opened and Dorothy Henry bustled in. Her ample frame was tucked in a silky blouse and her disapproving gaze landed on him.

"What are you doing here?" she snapped.

"Visiting my uncle." Cody tried to sound in charge, but Dorothy's eyes were like little lasers, cutting him to her size.

"You should go now. He needs his rest," she said as she cleared away Ted's soup bowl and napkin. "And for your information, I heard what you said. Vivienne Clayton is staying at Brooke's house. She isn't in Denver at all, and she looks terrible, I might say. Saw her sitting on Brooke's porch the other day looking positively wrung out." She turned and her eyes impaled him, as if accusing him of being the cause of Vivienne's distress.

Cody frowned. "What do you mean, not in Denver?"

Dorothy waved an imperious hand at him, as if to dismiss him. "I mean what I said. She's still in Clayton."

Cody shot a frown at Ted, who was looking distinctly smug. "You should probably check this out for yourself," Ted said, throwing back the covers. "And I'm getting out of bed. High time I did something on this place."

"Mr. Struthers, you are certainly not well enough to be up and about," Dorothy chided, putting down the half-empty soup bowl as if to stop him.

Cody didn't wait to see how this scenario played out. He zipped up his coat and dropped his hat on his head, questions dogging him as he strode out the door.

Vivienne was still hanging around Clayton because of the inheritance. That was all.

He tried to stifle his thoughts and wonderings, but as he got caught up on his paperwork, paid some bills, prepared ear tags for the calves and went over his fall checklist for the cattle, he couldn't get the picture of Vivienne Dorothy created out of his mind. Positively wrung out? Why?

And when Bonnie came home from school, sullen and cranky, complaining that she had to help Delores with the cooking and why couldn't Cody see that Vivienne really cared about him and why couldn't Cody go and get her, Cody had had enough.

If Vivienne was still in Clayton, he needed to know exactly why, he figured as he got into his truck, started it up and headed downtown. Besides, he still owed her some money. And he had to find Bryce and have a little chat with him. And talk to Art about the butcher job they did on Vivienne's brakes.

He wasn't running after Vivienne Clayton at all. Not at all.

"I know it's hard to think about, and I know you've had your own struggles with the Clayton family, but could you think of coming?" Vivienne clutched the handset of the phone, waiting for Mei's response.

She gave Brooke's swing a push with the toe of her shoe, the rhythmic swinging easing some of her tension away. It had taken her a couple of days to connect with Mei, and she wasn't sure what kind of reception her cousin would give her. At the funeral, Mei had been polite but distant. And now, she sounded much the same.

"So did your P.I. tell you why Lucas didn't come to the reading of the will?" Mei sounded distracted. "Are you sure he wasn't simply being his usual rebellious self?"

"He told us that a man fitting Lucas's description has kidnapped a child. We think he took the boy from some drug dealers down in the Everglades. The P.I. thinks the drug dealers are now are after Lucas and the little boy."

Vivienne heard Mei's sharp intake of breath and she waited while her cousin digested this news.

"Does anyone…know if he's okay?"

"As far as we know he is." Vivienne switched the phone to her other hand, her own concern over Lucas, for now, overshadowing the other sorrows in her life. "But we're only hearing sketchy reports." She gave the swing another push, wondering if she dared ask Mei to come back to Clayton. At the funeral, only a couple of the cousins made a strong commitment to coming back. Lucas wasn't there, and Mei didn't seem convinced she wanted to return.

But Vivienne couldn't fault her. At one time she wasn't sure she wanted to return herself.

And now she wished she hadn't. Because coming back had meant meeting Cody. Coming back had meant falling hard for a cowboy who didn't seem to care that she was gone.

Her heart contracted at the thought of Cody, and she brushed her own aching feelings aside. For now she wanted to concentrate on Mei and what she needed.

"So I'm guessing you want me to return," Mei said, her voice sharp.

"It would be wonderful if we could be together. If we could pray together," Vivienne said. "I think now, more than ever, we need to be a family. To pray for Lucas and to support each other."

More silence, then Mei eased out a sigh. "I know. I know. I've…I've missed you all, as well."

Her admission warmed Vivienne's chilled heart. "I'm glad to hear that," she said quietly.

They talked a bit more. Vivienne brought her up to speed on what was going on in Clayton but didn't give her much information about what she was doing herself.

What could she tell her cousin other than she was wandering around Clayton, looking for a job? Looking for some way to keep busy while she nursed her broken heart. When Vivienne had come to Clayton, her dreams were crystal clear. Stay around for her required year then go back to New York and start her restaurant.

Trouble was, it wasn't what she wanted anymore.

She thought of her family and the connections they'd rebuilt. She thought of the renewal her faith had undergone while living here. Could she really leave that behind? A reluctant smile played across her lips. Her grandfather probably anticipated this when he thought of this scheme.

Vivienne picked up the Bible she had sitting on the other side. She'd had lots of time to read it lately. And she'd been finding comfort in the words of the Psalms. Today it was Psalm 31.

"…as for me, I trust in the LORD. I will be glad and rejoice in your love, for you saw my affliction and knew the anguish of my soul."

Vivienne stopped there, rereading the words and letting them take root in her heart. God knew what she was going through right now, and while she knew so many people had so much more to deal with than broken hearts and bad mistakes, she still needed the comfort God's word could give her right now.

She covered her face in her hands. "Help me to truly trust in You, Lord," she prayed. "Help me not to think that my work is more important than

You. Help me to remember that my heart belongs to You." She stopped as that very heart clenched in sorrow. She knew God was faithful and that He would comfort her, but at the same time she knew her sadness over Cody would not leave her quickly.

He had become so much a part of her that being away from him, only these few days, caused deep sorrow and pain. She missed him. She cared for him more than she had cared for anyone else.

She loved him.

The thought struck her like a jolt. Then she closed her eyes. Too late. Too late.

She knew she couldn't go back to the ranch. She knew she didn't belong there. Hadn't that been made clear again and again? She let the horses out, Cody thought she cut the fence, she had almost killed his men with her cooking. She didn't belong on the ranch. She'd never make a ranch wife.

Useless.

And Cody hadn't even bothered to call her. To talk to her.

I'll never go after another woman again.

So why should he come after her? He didn't need her.

"Dear Lord, help me to trust in You and You alone. Help me to love You first," she prayed, slowly releasing her heart into the Lord's loving hands. Then she opened her Bible and began reading again.

She didn't look terrible but she did look sad.

And she obviously wasn't in Denver.

Cody stood at the end of the sidewalk leading up to Brooke's house, watching Vivienne pushing herself on the swing, her head bent, his questions and confusion battling with the welcome sight of her.

Her eyes were looking intently at a book in her lap. Instead of her usual silky blouses and narrow skirts, she wore blue jeans and an old flannel shirt. Her hair hung around her face, just how he liked it. She wore no makeup, and she looked like she'd been crying.

But she still looked fantastic.

His heart jumped in his chest with a combination of nerves and confusion. He thought for sure Dorothy Henry was wrong. That he was coming to Brooke's place on a wild goose chase.

He had put off coming here, not sure of how he would be received.

Please, Lord, he prayed, *give me the right words.*

But he did know that he cared for Vivienne more than he had ever cared for anyone else. That his days were empty without her. And that the longer he stood here, the harder it would be to tell her that.

He took a deep breath, sent up another quick prayer and walked up the sidewalk to the porch.

Vivienne turned a page in the book she was reading, the rustle of the paper the only sound in the quiet that settled on the neighborhood. It was as if everything waited—even Silver Creek, flowing behind the house, had quieted to a soothing murmur, waiting to hear what he had to say.

She sniffed, then wiped her nose with a soggy tissue. Then dabbed at her eyes with the same tissue. Her eyes were red and her cheeks pale.

He cleared his throat and her head flew up, her hair flowing back from her face. She slammed the book shut and dropped it on the seat beside her, then jumped to her feet.

"What…what are you doing… What do you want?" she stammered, her hand reaching for the door of the house. As if she was trying to get away from him.

Cody took a halting step closer, thinking of how he would handle a skittish horse, feeling as if he needed to use the same approach here.

"I just want to talk to you," he said quietly, raising one hand just a little. Making a tentative move in her direction.

"What about?" She sniffed again but lowered her hand.

"About us. About why you left. About why you're still here in Clayton."

She frowned. "Where else would I be?"

Her question threw him off. "Denver?" he offered.

"Why would I be in Denver?"

"Chef Andre? From Au something-or-other?" He couldn't help the edge entering his voice. "I forgot to pass the message on, but I'm sure he called again offering you a job."

"He did."

"And you didn't take it?" he queried.

"No. Why would I?"

"Because you were just there a week ago." He wasn't sure what to say or how to say it. "Didn't you apply for a job then?"

She shook her head. "No. I applied for that job a couple of months ago. When I came back after getting fired in New York."

"So that wasn't the reason you went to Denver last weekend?"

"I went to buy supplies for your birthday dinner." Vivienne's frown deepened. "How did you know about the job?" she continued.

Cody felt sheepish, but behind his embarrassment was a jolt of relief at her admission.

A couple of months ago, he told himself. She applied for that job a couple of months ago. She had gone to Denver to buy supplies for his birthday dinner.

But he forced his attention back to her question. "I answered your phone. When I was driving your car back from the auto repair shop. Mine was dead and I thought maybe someone from the ranch was trying to call me. And it was this chef guy offering you a job. I thought you wanted to leave. That you wanted to go back to being a real chef in a real restaurant. Not living on the ranch."

Vivienne wrapped her arms around her midsection, but she hadn't made a move toward the house. Or toward him.

"I heard you had an accident with my car. When you drove it back to the ranch."

Cody pushed down a flicker of frustration at her comment. Her car. Her job. This wasn't what he wanted to talk to her about, but he figured he had better work his way slowly to the real reason he was here. "I just came back from Art Krueger's. He looked over the car and said the brake line had been nicked. So it leaked fluid. Which made the brakes fail. He suspects Billy Dean had something to do with it because shortly after I picked up the car, Billy Dean quit."

"Are you okay?" The concern in her voice ignited a glimmer of hope.

"I'm fine. But I reported the incident. I'm sure the other Claytons had something to do with it, as well." And when he reported the incident he had to put up with Sheriff Zach's cool attitude. As if it was his fault Vivienne was sitting on a porch with red eyes, reading the Bible. And maybe it was. "I'm pretty sure the other Claytons had something to do with the food poisoning, as well," he added.

What little color Vivienne had left in her face drained away at the mention of that horrible incident. She held her hands in front of her as if pushing away what he might have to say. "That was so horrible. People could have died."

"Uncle Ted saw Bryce in the kitchen. Fooling with the soup," Cody hurriedly explained, hoping to catch her midflight. "And Bryce and Billy Dean were pretty tight. I'm convinced they were all involved with Bryce putting something in the soup that made everyone sick. I think they were trying to do to you what has been happening to your cousins. I think they're trying to get you to leave."

Vivienne pressed her hand to her mouth and she looked away, as if hardly daring to believe what he was saying.

Cody was encouraged by her response and took another step closer. Now he was directly in front of her. He tossed his hat on the glider and gently cupped her shoulders in his hands.

"It wasn't your fault, Vivienne. You didn't make anyone sick."

"But…I let it happen." Her comment was a feeble protest, and Cody lifted her chin so he could look into her eyes.

"How could you know what Bryce would do?"

Then, finally, her gaze swerved up and locked on his. "Do you believe that?"

He frowned, wondering where that question had come from. "Of course I do. You're an amazing cook—chef," he corrected, wanting to get things right. "You would never be that careless. And I'm pretty sure Bryce, Billy Dean and who knows who else have all been involved in some of the other things that went on at the ranch." He thought of Bryce's insidious comments about Vivienne and his veiled implication that Vivienne had somehow been involved in the cutting of the fence.

"And Cade?" she asked.

"He wasn't involved in any of it. Seems to me and Uncle Ted that Bryce just set him up as the fall guy. I talked to Cade and I believe him when he said he wasn't involved. It wouldn't make any sense for him to alienate a family he wanted to be a part of."

"He's a nice guy," Vivienne admitted. "And if he was at fault, I doubt he would have stayed around once everything was discovered."

Cody gave an impatient nod, eager to move on to more important things.

Vivienne looked away, moisture shining from one corner of her eye, and when she blinked, it tracked down her cheek. He removed it with one thumb, his heart turning over at the relief on her features.

"And I never got to thank you for making my birthday dinner." He lowered his voice, hoping to reconnect with her.

She looked up, hope shimmering in her eyes. "I wanted to make your day special," she said quietly, dashing at another tear trickling down her face. "And it turned out so badly. I felt like such a failure. I'd made so many mistakes on the ranch. I felt like I didn't belong there."

"Like I said, not your fault." Then as her words registered, realization dawned. "Was that what you were talking about when you said you were useless? That you couldn't be at the ranch? That you had to leave?"

Vivienne nodded, her gaze slipping away from his, as if reliving her shame. "I couldn't seem to do things right."

He cupped her face in both his hands and turned her again to face him.

"Why would you ever think that? What would ever make you think that?"

Her eyes flicked up to his but then settled on his chest. "I let the horses out. Bryce made it sound like you thought it was my fault the cows got out. I couldn't even go for a walk and not almost sprain my ankle in those stupid city boots. And then, the one thing I thought I could do got messed up." She looked up at him again. "I really, truly felt like a city girl. I loved the ranch so much and I wanted so badly to belong…to be someone who could help you…to be…" Her words faded away as her gaze lowered again.

"You wanted to belong?" He tried to make the words fit into the black thoughts he'd been harboring the past few days. Thoughts of Vivienne wanting to leave. To get as far away from the ranch—and him—as possible. "You love the ranch?"

"I didn't want to be like Tabitha. I wanted to be someone who could be a partner to you."

Cody felt a rush of affection and behind that a deeper, stronger emotion he couldn't express in words.

So he bent his head to hers and caught her lips with his in a deep, satisfying kiss. He wrapped his arms around her, holding her close to his heart.

Then he pressed his lips to her cheek, her neck, nestling her head against his shoulder. "I can't believe I got it so wrong," he murmured. "I thought you'd had enough of the ranch and you wanted to leave as fast as possible. I thought you had enough of me."

Vivienne pressed her face against his coat, her

arms wrapped tightly around him. "No, never enough of you. I thought I was nothing but trouble to you. Just a mistake." She pulled away, her eyes shining with tears, but with something more. With joy and happiness. "I love the ranch, and I love you. I didn't want to go, but I thought I was just making things worse for you."

"The only way you make things worse for me is by leaving me all alone."

She swallowed and then reached up and ran her hand over the stubble on his chin. "And you came after me."

"I'm sorry it took so long." He dropped another kiss on her mouth, as if hoping, by that action, to atone for his tardiness. "I was so sure you were gone. That you left for Denver."

"I wanted to come back to the ranch so many times, but I was too ashamed." She gave him a tentative smile. "And I knew you said you would never go after a girl again, so I knew you wouldn't come after me."

"I didn't deserve to have you back at the ranch. Not the way I jumped to conclusions." He stroked her face with his hand. "I'm so sorry for all the mistakes I made. So sorry for ever thinking what I did."

"If the other Claytons were involved, you were probably getting fed lots of poisonous tidbits."

"I should have known better. I should have

trusted you." He sighed, then he brushed his lips over her forehead, his eyes drifting shut. "I love you, Vivienne Clayton. And I want you to come back to the ranch with me. And I want you to make the move permanent."

Vivienne grew utterly still.

"Did I hear you right?" she whispered.

Cody drew back and gave her a tentative smile. "I hope you did." Then he brushed her hair away from her face, kissed her again and said, "I want you to marry me."

"Are you sure?"

"As sure as I've ever been of anything in my life."

She gazed up at him. "But do you think I'll fit in?"

"The huge hole in my heart says that you fit in very well," Cody said, his voice rough with emotion.

"Okay. I want to be with you," she said quietly. "But don't say I didn't warn you."

"I don't need to be warned. I just need to know whether you will or not."

Vivienne rose up on her tiptoes, caught her hand behind Cody's neck and gave him a gentle kiss. "I will," she whispered.

The weight Cody had been carrying since Vivienne left shifted off his shoulders. He wanted to laugh. To swing her around and to proclaim to anyone who would listen that Vivienne Clayton was his lady.

Instead he pulled her close. "I suppose we'll have to tell your family," he said quietly. "I'm sure Zach will want to know what's happening. He gave me the evil eye when I stopped in there to let him know about your car."

Vivienne pulled away, drawing him to the swing. They sat down together, but she kept her hands twined in his. "I'm sure you will. He can be a bit of a father bear at times."

Cody stroked her face again. "So you really want to move to the ranch?"

"I do," she said quietly.

"And what about your dream of owning your own restaurant?"

Vivienne gave him a trembling smile. "It's not as important as being with you."

He believed her answer was true, but he also knew that he had learned something from Tabitha. He didn't want Vivienne to lose herself in the ranch. To lose the dreams that he knew were as much a part of her as her blond hair and blue eyes.

He gave a push on the swing, the creaking of the chains the only sound in the following silence. "Remember how I was so worried you would turn the ranch into a retreat?"

She laughed at that, laying her head on his shoulder. "It didn't happen, did it?"

"But it could."

She went still at that.

Cody ran his fingers over hers, tracing their lines, finding the scar from when she had hurt herself that morning they had made breakfast together. A few other nicks and scars dotted her hands. He guessed that someone who made their living wielding knives would suffer a few cuts from time to time.

"I was thinking that you've got all these amazing skills and talents and you had your dreams. I'd like to find a way for you to use them. On the ranch. I was thinking we could have a retreat. Where people could come to the ranch and enjoy the outdoors and eat amazing food."

Vivienne went utterly still at that. "But wouldn't that interfere with the working of the ranch?" Her voice was quiet, as if speaking too loudly might break the moment.

Cody shrugged, stroking her fingers. "We could make it part of the working of the ranch. I went on the internet and saw that there are other ranches that have people come and stay and help with some of the basic ranch chores. Kind of like you did when you came on that cattle drive. You'd never done it before."

"It was fun."

"And at the end of the day if guests could sit down to a gourmet cooked meal..." He didn't finish the sentence, hoping her imagination would fill in the rest.

"And I could do some catering from time to time."

"You have your first gig doing Cade and Jasmine's wedding. Once word gets out, you might have more work than you know what to do with."

Vivienne lifted her head from Cade's shoulder, her eyes sparkling with a life that Cody had never seen before. "If we do this, I could use the money Grandpa George willed to me. I could use it to help bring more business to Clayton. We could have different events." She turned to him, her shining eyes making him love her even more, if that was possible.

He smiled in return, his heart overflowing with thanks.

"Maybe a dance," he said, tracing her features with his finger. "And maybe I'll ask the girl I'm crazy about to come with me."

To his surprise, Vivienne blushed. She looked down. "I was a silly girl for turning you down in high school," she murmured. "I wonder what my life would have been like if I had said yes then."

He brushed a kiss over her forehead. "It doesn't really matter now, does it? We're together now and I have no regrets."

"That's a good way to live."

"It's how I hope and pray we can carry on. And with God's help, I'm sure we will."

She nestled against him and eased out a sigh. "Me, too."

Cody held her close and gave the swing a push, and the creaking of the chains kept time with the satisfying words running through his head.

Vivienne and Cody. Together at last.

* * * * *

LARGER-PRINT BOOKS!

GET 2 FREE LARGER-PRINT NOVELS PLUS 2 FREE MYSTERY GIFTS

Larger-print novels are now available...

YES! Please send me 2 FREE LARGER-PRINT Love Inspired® novels and my 2 FREE mystery gifts (gifts are worth about $10). After receiving them, if I don't wish to receive any more books, I can return the shipping statement marked "cancel". If I don't cancel, I will receive 6 brand-new novels every month and be billed just $4.99 per book in the U.S. or $5.49 per book in Canada. That's a saving of at least 23% off the cover price. It's quite a bargain! Shipping and handling is just 50¢ per book in the U.S. and 75¢ per book in Canada.* I understand that accepting the 2 free books and gifts places me under no obligation to buy anything. I can always return a shipment and cancel at any time. Even if I never buy another book, the two free books and gifts are mine to keep forever.

122/322 IDN FEG3

Name _____ (PLEASE PRINT)

Address _____ Apt. # _____

City _____ State/Prov. _____ Zip/Postal Code _____

Signature (if under 18, a parent or guardian must sign)

Mail to the **Reader Service:**
IN U.S.A.: P.O. Box 1867, Buffalo, NY 14240-1867
IN CANADA: P.O. Box 609, Fort Erie, Ontario L2A 5X3

Not valid to current subscribers to Love Inspired Larger-Print books.

**Are you a current subscriber to Love Inspired books
and want to receive the larger-print edition?
Call 1-800-873-8635 or visit www.ReaderService.com.**

LILP11B

Love Inspired® SUSPENSE

RIVETING INSPIRATIONAL ROMANCE

Watch for our series of edge-
of-your-seat suspense novels.
These contemporary tales
of intrigue and romance
feature Christian characters
facing challenges to their faith...
and their lives!

AVAILABLE IN REGULAR
& LARGER-PRINT FORMATS

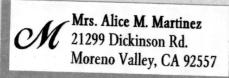